DATE DUE   JUL 05

| 3-13-06 | | | |
|---|---|---|---|
| | | | |
| | | | |
| | | | |
| | | | |
| | | | |
| | | | |
| | | | |
| | | | |
| | | | |
| | | | |
| | | | |
| | | | |
| | | | |
| | | | |
| | | | |
| | | | |
| | | | |
| | | | |

# FIRE
# IN THE
# DESERT

*Also by D. B. Newton
in Large Print:*

Border Graze
Hideout Valley
The Oregon Rifles
Ambush Reckoning
Born to the Brand
Bullet Lease
Crooked River Canyon
The Lurking Gun
The Oxbow Deed
Shotgun Freighter

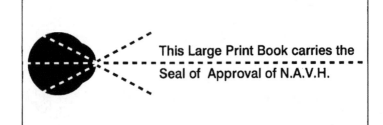

This Large Print Book carries the
Seal of Approval of N.A.V.H.

# 1

Corey woke, to the hand tugging at his sleeve. "Steve! *Steve!*" Melissa Tyler's voice urgently calling his name dragged him slowly out of a fagged sleep and he opened his eyes.

Sweltering July heat was trapped here beneath the wagon cover; the smear of sunlight on canvas dazzled him and made him raise a shading arm across his face. He was drenched with sweat. Through his makeshift bed among burlap sacks that held grain for the teams, he could feel the hard jostling of the wagon's slow-turning wheels.

He groaned a little and then, as Melissa spoke his name again, hauled himself onto an elbow and turned to find the Mormon girl kneeling beside him, her strong hands laid along her thighs. "What it is?"

"Sioux!" she whispered. "Orson thinks so anyway. Yonder."

She pointed. Quickly Corey rolled over and pushed up the lower edge of the wagon canvas for a look. Beyond a sunshimmer of tawny sage flats, low hills danced in the heated air. A dry watercourse, willow-lined, margined them. Steve Corey studied the scene during a long moment, eyes narrowed as the sun reached through the opening between canvas and wagon to strike his brown, unsmiling face.

Melissa said, "Is it?" There was no needless panic in her, he knew; she would wait for his decision, and meanwhile her brown eyes rested on him with a trust and confidence that touched and yet somehow irritated him.

"Might be." He nodded, shortly. "These mules of ours are a prime target. More than one mail courier on this Laramie route has lost his scalp and teams!" On his knees he reached for belt and holster that had been laid aside for comfort as he slept. He flipped them into place about his hips, thumbed home the prong of the buckle.

"What are you going to do?"

"Give them a chance to show what's on their minds." He pulled the Navy Colt and spun its cylinder, to check the loads and the seating of the caps upon the nipples. As he lowered the hammer of the heavy weapon and holstered it, he added, "*You* stay out of sight! If it's Indians, last thing they need to know is that there's a white woman in this hack!"

"Steve —"

His manner must have struck at her; her quick protest sounded hurt. He shrugged a little.

"All right," he said. "No use arguing. I made it clear to Brigham what I thought of the Church sending women out to these wilderness stations. I'm taking no responsibility."

"But you are, though." Something in her voice made him pause to glance at her. The heat had put a faint sheen of moisture across her flushed face; he saw that her soft, dark hair had been drawn into a knot, to keep it off the back of her neck. She wore a long skirt of homespun, and one of her brother's shirts, with sleeves rolled to the elbows and the collar unbuttoned and turned in. He could see the cleft of her swelling bosom, smell the good, personal scent of her warm flesh.

"You've been worrying about me," she told him, "all the way from Salt Lake. And you mustn't, Steve! I'll have my brother with me; I'll be all right. We're proud to be chosen for this work, and to go wherever our Church decides we're needed. I thought you understood."

Steve Corey said, "I guess I don't. Even a year of working to lay out this express line hasn't taught me as much as I'd like to know about you people. But I'm still trying!" He reached and covered one of her hands with his own. "Just forget what I said. I'm touchy, for some reason."

Her eyes smiled. "No wonder! You've been losing sleep! You thought I didn't know? I've looked out of the wagon and seen you, night after night, since we passed Echo Canyon — sitting there with your back against the wheel and your gun ready, watching over me. . . ."

The man's dark face softened, as he gave her hand a squeeze. "We'll be at the fort by nightfall. Maybe there I can get caught up." He added, and his manner was brusque again, "Tell Dan Fox to keep those mules in their collars, but not show any sign of fear. I'll have a look around."

She did not argue; as a pioneer woman she accepted a man's judgments without protest even if they led him into danger. Corey could feel her look follow him as he crawled to the rear gate of the mail hack where his horse, a sorrel mare, trailed under saddle. Untying the reins, he swung directly over and dropped upon its back.

He held up and let the wagon roll away,

its wheels and the hoofs of the four-mule team lifting tawny dust to streak its canvas and partly obliterate the letters stenciled on the side of the box: BRIGHAM YOUNG EXPRESS. Melissa was watching from the rear bow; Steve lifted an arm, then pulled his sorrel to the left and sent it at a long angle toward the line of dusty willows.

Farther west stood pine slopes and the shining spire of Laramie Peak. A sultry wind came up, sweeping through the sage and molding the sweaty shirt to Corey's long, hard-muscled torso. Wind ran across the willows, in a wave of light and dark. Then, in a break of the trees, he saw a rider pass briefly through sunlight and again into shadow.

The naked body shone copper, against the paint pattern of a saddleless horse. The Indian carried a long bow, but Corey saw no war paint on him, or on his pony; that was reassuring. Then, with an unexpected whir of wings a prairie hen exploded from the sage, thirty feet from him. Corey watched it rise, a swift blur. And on an impulse, his right hand was sweeping downward and catching up the cap-and-ball Navy from his open-top belt holster.

As the weapon came up his thumb found

the hammer spur, brought it back; his fore-finger touched trigger. The crack of the explosion made a flat, jarring sound in that immense stillness. White powder smoke spurted from gun muzzle; and the bird, plucked from the sky, plummeted into the sage. A lone feather swinging lazily on an eddy of heated air indicated where it had fallen.

With elaborate casualness, Steve Corey blew down the barrel of the gun to clear it and dropped it into holster. This was good shooting and he knew it; what was more important, the watching Sioux within the willows would know it, too. He kneed the mare forward and, dismounting, got the dead bird and rose again into saddle.

He examined with approval the work his ball had done — taking his target on the wing, striking it neatly without doing damage to the good flesh. Such shooting with a hand gun could only be a product of much spent powder, of many lonely hours of practice. Using a knuckle to push the hat back from his forehead, he lifted a glance toward the trees. Nothing stirred. A tight grin of satisfaction warped his mouth. Slinging his bird across the saddle pommel, Corey deliberately reined about and set his back to the willows, and clapping heels to dusty flanks struck off after the wagon.

Melissa was on the seat now, between her brother Orson, whose young good looks mirrored her own, and gruff Dan Fox, who held the ribbons of the four-mule team in his big hands. Pacing the turning of the wheels, Corey quickly told what he had seen. "They were buck Sioux, all right. Just itching to take a crack at these mules if they'd had the nerve."

Orson Tyler said, "We heard a shot."

Corey held up the bird. "Figured to remind them how straight a Colt would shoot. Much as they'd like to, I doubt they'll take a chance of jumping us — not this close to Fort Laramie."

"How much farther?" asked the girl.

He pointed ahead into the sunsmear. "Should be able to see it from that next rise. We'll lay over there tonight and go on to Bear Creek Station tomorrow."

Fox flipped the reins, and Corey pulled away again. A saddle felt good after the heat and jolting of the rig. The Sioux were still clinging to the willow cover — if in fact they hadn't already struck out for other places. As he rode, though, Corey kept a watch on that line of trees, for he knew the Indian's trickiness from long experience.

13

The ground was lifting under him now. Presently it fell away, and just below lay the level parade and the sod-roofed, wooden buildings of Fort Laramie. Two miles beyond, the confluence of the Laramie and the Platte made a smear of light reflecting the low sun. Hills rimmed the river bottoms, whose thick brown grasses held the long golden glow of afternoon — a busy scene, in this midsummer of 1857, the circled wagons of emigrant trains encamped, cattle grazing, and smoke rising from many campfires. As he watched, the clear voice of a trumpet floated across the other sounds, and the post flag began to crawl jerkily down its staff.

The last notes ran out and died upon the heated air, and Steve Corey spoke to his sorrel and heeled it ahead.

Nearer, he could see activity about those wagon camps; three separate trains, having covered the first leg of their journey from distant Missouri River ports, were laying over to make preparation for the last long haul that would take them on to Oregon or California. Here wagons would be taken apart and worn timbers carefully checked and replaced; loads would be shuffled and repacked, and things that had proved im-

14

practical discarded. In the proximity of the fort men and women could relax for a brief time after the vigil of the trail, to visit with the members of other camps and compare notes on the humor and tragedy of the crossing.

As he neared, a small spot of color in a swale a hundred yards or so from the closest of the camps caught his attention; he studied it idly and at last made out the checkered gingham of a child's apron. At the same moment he heard a woman's anxious call sounding across the stillness: "Sally! Sally Owen!" He saw the woman, beside a wheel of one of the wagons — a slender, long-skirted figure listening and getting no answer.

Frowning as he thought of the lurking Sioux, Corey reined toward that swale whose dip concealed it from the anxious searching of the woman. Long grass muffled his sorrel's hoofs and he was almost upon the child before she was aware of him, but she turned and looked up with no particular surprise.

"Hullo!"

She was a sunny-haired little girl, perhaps five years old and still retaining her baby chubbiness. She held a fistful of weeds, gathered under the impression they were flowers, and already wilting. Eyes as blue as the checks in her neatly laundered apron watched Corey rein in, lean his arm on the saddle pommel as he smiled down at her.

"Hello, Sally," he said pleasantly. "You suppose Mother's got your supper ready?"

The eyes widened. "How'd you know my name?"

"Guessed. I'm good at it. I make mistakes once in a while, but I never yet missed a Sally."

"Aw-w!" She was skeptical yet half convinced. She used a wrist to push corn-yellow hair back from her forehead.

"Want a ride?" he offered, reaching a hand down to her. "I bet this horse of mine could carry double. We'll tote you back to your wagon."

She took the hand trustingly and he lifted her from the ground with ease. "Take hold," he instructed. "And hang on good and tight. You set?"

"I — guess so!" She was a little breathless with the unfamiliar height, and the powerful surge of the mare's haunches under her; when the horse sprang forward, Corey felt the convulsive grip she tightened on his waist.

They pulled up beside a campfire, where

Steve Corey swung the little girl into her mother's waiting arms. "Here's Sally, Mrs. Owen," he said. "She got kind of far afield."

"Mommy," the child exclaimed, over-awed, "this man knows people's names just by looking at 'em!"

He showed the woman a quick grin, "It isn't guaranteed to work, ma'am."

She smiled in return, and set the child down. She was a young and pleasant woman, pretty, and berry-brown from weeks upon the trail. "I'm obliged to you," she told him, in a voice that held the tang of Middle-Western speech.

"I wouldn't want to scare you, but even this close to the fort it's not a good idea for youngsters to stray too far. You never can tell."

"I know. They're so active it's hard to keep track of them. I turned around for a minute and she'd disappeared."

Better, he decided, to say nothing about Indians lurking in the neighborhood; it would only cause alarm and there actually was little danger. The aroma from a big kettle on the fire caught his nostrils and he sniffed appreciatively. "Stew smells good," he told her. "You might try this in it, for a little flavor." He handed down the

17

prairie hen he had killed.

The woman's husband had come into sight around the end of the wagon — a tall, slow-moving young man, hands in the hip pockets of his overalls. "That's kind of you, stranger," he said in an easy drawl. "How about sharing supper with us? I'm Jess Owen. Ruth, here, is my missis. We're an Arkansas company, mostly — California bound. Train captain's name is Fancher."

Corey introduced himself, leaning from saddle to shake hands with the pair of them — the man's palm tough and calloused with the labor of farming, his wife's firm and strong. "Obliged to you," he said, "but I'm due at the fort. Just got in from Salt Lake with the mail wagon."

He noticed an abrupt change that came over these people. They still smiled, but a kind of distance settled between them. And the little girl, half hidden in her mother's skirts, suddenly blurted, "Is he a Mormon, Mommy? He looks like just anybody!"

Too late her mother cried, "Sally! Hush!"

Steve, puzzled and a little amused, said, "It's all right, ma'am. She's likely never seen a Mormon. I'm not one, but even if I was it wouldn't matter. You can take my word, Sally, they do look like just anybody. And some," he added, thinking of Melissa Tyler, "a lot better!"

"I'm afraid she's been hearin' talk," Owen explained apologetically. "Talk she can't be expected to understand. There's men from Missouri and Illinois with this train who brag about the part they had in running those people out of the States ten years ago. And now, with the army bein' sent against them —"

Corey stiffened. "What are you talking about? What army?"

The man and his wife exchanged a look. Ruth Owen cried, "Good land! Maybe they haven't even heard! Maybe they don't know about the trouble they're in!"

"Sure, there's been trouble," Corey said. "Brigham Young had a row with some worthless judge the federal government appointed, and sent him packing. That was three months ago, and ever since we've been waiting to see what would come of it."

"I'd say plenty's come of it!" the Arkansas emigrant told him bleakly. "This judge you spoke of went and complained to the President, and because of it Buchanan has declared Utah Territory to be in a state of rebellion. There's a new governor been named to replace Young, and when we left Kansas, troops were starting to concentrate at Fort Leavenworth. The expedition may have started west by this time!"

Shocked and stunned, Steve Corey slowly rubbed his jaw with the back of a fist, "I just don't understand! I know these people! There's been a hell of a mistake somewhere. . . ."

Then a burst of shouting caused his head to jerk. All around them men had dropped whatever they were doing and were running across the compound, heading for a point at the far edge of the wagon corral. Some excitement appeared to have broken out. Owen, shaking his head in disapproval, grunted, "Those Missouri wildcats, I suppose — fighting again!"

But Corey, standing in the stirrups, saw from his vantage point what the farmer could not see — the familiar shape of the mule wagon. An exclamation broke from him; at once he had dropped back into the saddle, and the sorrel lunged forward.

It was a fight, plain enough, from the sway and surge of the gathering crowd. When he struck the edge of it he kept right on, the emigrants scattering out of his sorrel's way. And there was young Orson

20

Tyler, trading blows with a big, overalled farmer who looked to have some thirty pounds' advantage of him.

Light-boned and slender, Tyler had no chance against such an adversary; his face was already bloodied and bruised, while the Missourian showed hardly any mark at all. Corey yelled, but his voice was lost as the swing of a heavy fist took the Mormon youth squarely in the face and drove him back, to smash against the side of the wagonbox. Melissa was on the seat, holding the reins and wearing a look of horror. Corey had this glimpse of her as the big man waded in to finish off his stunned and helpless victim. Then Corey's sorrel struck the farmer and sent him rolling.

At the same moment Dan Fox got to young Tyler to help him to his feet. "Stop it!" shouted Steve Corey, and his words brought an uneasy stillness. "What is this, Dan?"

Dan Fox was a stolid, methodical workhorse of a man in his early thirties, a few years older than Corey himself, a man to rely on. He wagged his big head toward the scowling farmers. "These men stopped the wagon, as we tried to go past. They sounded drunk to me. They made some remarks —"

"They said things," Tyler broke in, "not fit for my sister or any decent woman to hear!"

Someone said, "A hell of a lot of respect the likes of you could have for a decent woman! Harem-keepin' sons of —"

"We'll have no more of that talk!" said a new voice. "Not while I'm running this train!"

Steve Corey looked over at the man who had pushed his way through the press. He was another emigrant like the rest, and his eyes held a worried pucker that suggested the job of train captain might be a little more than he could handle. Steve said crisply, "Are you Fancher?"

"Who would you be?"

"That don't matter. The important thing is, you're taking this outfit straight into Mormon territory. If your people don't want trouble, they'll watch their tongues. You understand what I'm saying?"

One of the crowd gave a hoot that had liquor behind it. "I figure to get along just fine with them Mormons! Maybe they'll lend me some of their spare women, I can start me a harem of my own. Wouldn't mind a damn bit beginning on that one right there on the wagon —"

Stung to fury, Steve found himself half

way out of saddle — but for once Dan
Fox had moved more quickly than he.
Blunt, honest face gone white, Dan
whirled on the speaker. His fist started
from the hip, with all Dan's broad-
shouldered power behind it. To the thud
of the blow, the Missourian buckled and
went back into the arms of his friends,
knocked cold.

Corey settled back, still trembling with
anger. Only the tightness about the mouth
showed Dan's feelings as he turned away,
flexing the fingers of his bruised hand.
Looking at him, Corey suddenly felt the
probing of a wholly unexpected thought: *Is
he in love with Melissa?* Strange, how you
could know a man well and yet not antici-
pate the surprising things he was capable
of.

Dan Fox had never, in his stolid way,
given any hint of the feelings that might lie
deep inside him; but they showed in his
eyes as he looked at the girl upon the
wagon seat, then quickly away again — almost as though what he had done was
somehow shameful.

Corey put a hand on Orson Tyler's
shoulder and turned him toward the
wagon. "Climb up!" he ordered. "Let's get
out of this!"

He put his glance over the crowd, but he saw no danger in them. A kind of stunned awe lay upon them and for the moment nobody moved or spoke. Satisfied, Steve prodded his sorrel and the mare moved ahead, as Dan Fox took the reins from Melissa and gave the mules a slap with the leather. In a dead silence the wagon rolled on, toward the fort.

Once Steve Corey hipped about for another look at the wagon camp. The crowd was dispersing, returning to the various supper fires whose pencil lines of smoke rose lazily. The circle of wagons with the homely clutter of household things about them presented once more a very peaceful scene.

Steve thought of the Owens — good, friendly people, deserving of the best at the end of their long trek to a new home in California. But there were also those Missourians, belligerent troublemakers; and the good-intentioned but not too competent captain of the train, with the worried pucker about his eyes and the responsibility for somehow welding all these into a functioning unit and getting them to their goal. Perhaps Fancher could do the trick, and avoid more trouble than that which had broken out this afternoon . . . perhaps not.

Corey wished him well and then dismissed him, his thoughts returning darkly to the news that he had heard.

# 2

A few clouds that hung above the western hills were coppery with sunset now, and the face of the river reflected back those colors. Since 1834, under one name or another, a fort had stood here on the bank of the Laramie, first as a trading post of the Rocky Mountain Fur Company, then as an outfitting point for Oregon-bound trains, and during the last eight years as a full-fledged outpost of the army of the frontier. The original adobe stockade had long since been outgrown; the neat new parade flanked by stables, barracks, and officers' quarters lay hard by, on level ground beside the river.

Now, in the relaxed period between retreat and supper call, Fort Laramie had the look of any military post during off-duty. Troopers lounged around the barracks stoops or crossed the drill field toward the sutler's store. Voices drifted from open windows of quarters and kitchens; a horse whinnied in its stall. Two women stood talking on the shadowed veranda of married officers' quarters.

Steve Corey caught up with the wagon as it reached the encampment's edge. The effect of his beating seemed to be taking hold of young Tyler, for he sat with eyes closed and head leaning back against the wagon bow while his sister dabbed at his smashed lip with her handkerchief. One side of his face appeared to be shaping up into a dark bruise.

Corey asked, "How's he making out?"

"All right, I think."

"We can have the post surgeon take a look, in case there's need of stitches."

Tyler shook his head impatiently. "I'm all right." He straightened on the seat to look at Corey. "You have any idea what it was I heard some of them saying? Something about an army?"

Steve evaded the question. "Let's find MacLeod and talk to him; he should know. Perhaps there's word from Bishnell, in Independence."

At the far end of Officers' Row stood the adobe that housed the sutler's store and post office, a place kept busy by both trooper and emigrant. As they pulled up before the low, sod-roofed structure, Andrew MacLeod himself was standing in the doorway, and at once came out to greet them. Steve Corey thought the sutler's dour Scottish face held an even soberer look than usual.

He reached up to shake hands with the man in the saddle. "You already know Dan Fox," Steve said. "This is Orson Tyler and his sister. They're being sent out to Bear Creek Station to help with the relays and the emigrant trains." MacLeod's shrewd blue eyes took in the state of the young man's bloody face, but he withheld comment.

Instead he told the girl, with open approval of her good looks, "I'm fair pleased to meet ye, miss. Danny, take this trap yonder to the house. Mrs. MacLeod will have a place for Miss Tyler to stay the night, and we'll be wanting all of ye for supper. Eli Bishnell is here. It looks like we've got some things to talk about."

Corey nodded soberly. "Looks like we have!"

An hour later, they sat on the porch of the sutler's white frame house and watched the lights beginning across the encampment, and the fires of the emigrant trains; overhead the stars burned brighter in the wide sky. A somber quiet lay over them all. Eli Bishnell, a stern, thin man who had been Brigham's representative at Independence for the new express route, had told them everything that had been happening in the East; his report confirmed, in more detail, what Steve Corey had already pieced together.

"Aye, these are bad times," MacLeod said, into the stillness. "Hard to tell what to make of it all." The old Scot was trimming shavings from a tobacco plug into the smoke-blackened pipe between his knees. "I've heard whispers," he went on, "even in this lonely outpost. They say Buchanan is shaking in his boots, first because of the Kansas trouble, and now on account of the showing this new abolitionist party made in last year's election.

"If the Black Republicans should win in 'Sixty, 'tis said the South will surely quit the Union. Meanwhile there's some that figure the real purpose of this little military show is to get the army out of the way and keep it there, leaving no force to stop Buchanan's section from seceding. if things ever come to a real break."

"And we're to be the scapegoats!" cried Orson Tyler, hotly. "We're to see their army march into Deseret, looting and raping and killing —"

MacLeod put away his knife, tamped the bowl of his pipe with a broad thumb.

"Weel, now," he said patiently, "they tell us, laddie, that this is no but a peaceable occupying force that's coming. They count on the Saints to accept it, reasonable-like, without any need of fighting."

"They'll be in for the surprise of their lives, then! They want to oust Brigham Young and set some Gentile over us as governor — and put that worthless Amberson back on the bench to run our courts! They want to persecute us, the way they did back in '46 when we lived among them.

"Well, there's thirty thousand of us now," Orson Tyler continued, "enough to stretch a wall of guns across Echo Canyon they'll never batter down. And if they should, we'll fight them to the last man, woman, and child!"

Melissa said anxiously, "Orson! Please!" and at her quieting tone her brother broke off. The silence that followed was filled with his angry breathing.

Corey knew that what the young man had said held an ominous warning. Orson Tyler was a hothead, of course, but there was a strong taint of fanaticism among the Saints, bred of their long persecutions. Many would feel exactly as he, and stand ready to combat anything they saw as a hostile invasion by Gentile enemies.

But there would be others, too, like Dan Fox, who said now in his quiet and reasoned way, "Surely things haven't gone so far we can't do something to settle this trouble! After all, word hasn't even had time to reach Salt Lake. When the Fathers of the Church learn what's going on —"

"The army will be here before then," Bishnell interrupted. "When I left Missouri, there were twenty-five hundred troops under Colonel Johnston ready to take the road from Leavenworth. The first contingents are probably not far behind me."

"Aye," murmured MacLeod, "and in that case I fear it's too late to think of them turning back. Ye ken that these things have a momentum of their own." A sulphur match snapped alight under the Scot's thumbnail. He held it until the oily purple flame cleared and turned yellow, then put it to the bowl of his pipe and pulled the tobacco aglow.

"I still haven't told you all of it," Eli Bishnell continued. "The B. Y. has lost its mail contract — annulled by the government."

"That's impossible!" cried Steve Corey. "They'd have to have cause!"

"So they found one! The Gentile who held the contract before we underbid him has put his voice into the clamor against us. He says he has proof the mails have been tampered with at Salt Lake. It's a lie, of course, but with the mood this country is in, there's absolutely nothing we can do.

"I've already closed the office in Independence, and canceled all orders for stocking the stations that you built for us. A year's labor and expense gone for nothing!" He lifted his hands tiredly, let them drop again to the arms of his chair. "The first casualty of this situation!"

It was much more than that. Corey, stunned, thought of all it had meant, this far-seeing plan of the Mormon leaders to found an express company, and create a fast and dependable carrying service such as the West had never had. Success would have served to bind the nation more firmly together, would have brought the Pacific Coast weeks nearer to the East, so that at last a man could send an important document overland and have some assurance that it would reach its destination.

Corey thought of the months of preparation, the stations he had helped to lay out between here and the Missouri border, each stocked with relay teams and manned by fearless people like the Tylers. And now, on the verge of completion, all this must be scrapped.

Dan Fox said heavily, "Then — what are we to do?"

Young Tyler was on his feet, a tense silhouette against the starry darkness. "What we'll do, we'll turn the wagon around and head back to the Valley as fast as those mules will take us! Our people have got to be warned!"

Corey levered himself out of the rawhide-bottomed chair. He stood looking around him at the somber faces that were only dimly visible in the night. He could well imagine the impact this news would have when it reached the settlement at Deseret.

He felt suddenly tired and dispirited.

"You'll want an early start," he said. "And you'll be wanting to travel light in order to make time. I'm going on; the job I was hired for is finished. I'll take a pack-horse with me, and the mail we brought with us from Salt Lake; that, at least, we can know will get to Independence on schedule!"

They had all risen now, the talking ended. There was no more to be said. Corey heard the rustle of Melissa's skirts, and then she was close beside him, her hand touching his arm; but when he turned to her she suddenly whirled away without speaking and hurried into the house. A moment later, her brother and Dan Fox and Eli Bishnell were gone, and there was only the darkness, and the tramp of boots of a guard detachment crossing the parade.

"Stay a bit, lad," Andrew MacLeod told him. "Step in a minute. I've something for ye."

Corey followed his host inside. The Scot found a lamp and got it burning. The living room was a small one, its simple furnishings partly of local manufacture and partly bought from emigrants, a small portion only having been expensively freighted by bull train from the Missouri. MacLeod opened a cupboard and took from it a sealed envelope that bore Corey's name.

"Came last week," he said, "addressed to you here at the fort." Steve took it, knowing before he saw the Leavenworth postmark who had sent this letter; he had long been familiar with that precise and careful writing. "Go ahead and read it, if ye like," MacLeod invited. "I'll fetch the glasses, if ye'll join me in a little drink?"

Tearing open the envelope, Corey merely shook his head, and MacLeod smiled as he

34

took glass and bottle from the cupboard. "Aye, living among the Saints must have changed your habits. They are a prosperous people, for whom I have no but respect. Yet a wee drop and a pipeful, on occasion, never that I can see hurt anyone!" He poured and took his whisky, with a murmur of satisfaction.

Corey had finished reading; he folded the letter, frowning.

"Bad news?" MacLeod asked.

"No, as a matter of fact it's an offer of a job."

The trader lifted an eyebrow. "Oh? Well, I'd say ye could likely use one, your arrangement with Brigham having blown up so sudden-like."

"I suppose. This is from my old boss, Martin Wilcox, that took me as a green kid and gave me my first job skinning mule teams on his trains to Sante Fe. Later he upped me to wagonmaster — taught me everything he could. He was one of the biggest men in the trade, then; but I'm afraid the last few years he's been finding the going pretty hard."

"Aye. A good and honest businessman, perhaps not too practical at times. Still, things must have improved with him, since he's offering ye a position."

"They must for a fact. He says he's expanding and hopes to clear fifty thousand dollars this season. But one thing I don't understand. He's taken on a partner, someone named Baggett. Heard of him?"

"Never," said the Scot, after reflecting. "He can no be in freighting or I'd at least have heard the name. Perhaps some Easterner, with capital?"

"Maybe. Anyhow, the partnership has managed to land some valuable military contracts that will require buying a great deal of new rolling stock and equipment, and hiring wagon crews."

"Sounds like an opportunity ye can no afford to pass up, lad!"

"Not if he needs my help." Corey nodded soberly, stuffing the letter into a pocket of his shirt. "But I wish I knew more about this business arrangement. Martin Wilcox has always put too much trust in strangers."

"And there's such a thing as having a suspicious nature."

"True enough. I know nothing at all about this York Baggett, good or bad. Still, something strikes me wrong about these army contracts. Wilcox is hardly the man you'd think they'd choose for a job as important as hauling the supplies for

Johnston's expedition —"

"Oh, no, Steve!"

Both turned quickly, toward the hall leading into the back of the house. Melissa Tyler came another step into the room, her eyes holding Corey's in a look of consternation.

"I didn't mean to listen," she said. "But I heard; I couldn't help it. And you're turning against us, too? You, Steve Corey?"

"That isn't so, Melissa!"

She went on as though she hadn't heard. "We couldn't have asked or expected you to take our side in this trouble — not against your own people, your own government. But somehow I hadn't thought you'd actually help our enemies. You, of all men!"

There was no anger in her voice, merely a tired despair. Corey, trying to frame the words to answer her, heard MacLeod clear his throat indecisively. The Scot said, "Nay, lass! Ye mustn't think —"

Corey looked over at him. "Could we have a minute?"

Nodding in understanding, MacLeod put down his empty glass and reached for the pipe he had laid aside. Corey heard his step across to the door, heard it close behind him. Alone then, the man and the girl turned to face each other in the soft gleam of the lamp, her eyes reproachful, his pleading.

"Melissa —"

Suddenly, without warning, she was in his arms — her head pressed against him, her arms tight about his waist. He felt the frightened sobs that shook her. "You mustn't cry, honey! We don't know . . . maybe it won't come to anything."

They had never been like this. He caressed the dark smoothness of her hair. Then she pulled away; hands upon his shoulders, she lifted her eyes to his and her sweet face held a troubled, questioning look. "Be honest with me, Steve. Do you think less of me because I'm — because of my beliefs?"

"What kind of a question is that?" he exclaimed. "Who am I to judge any person's religion? And what difference could it make between us?"

She shook her head. "I feel sometimes as though there is a gulf that can't be bridged."

"Don't ever think that!" And as she started to turn her head away he caught her, forced her eyes to meet his own. "Melissa! Do you love me?"

Her warm lips trembled with the answer; then her eyes misted and she drew away from him. "I don't know!" Her voice was muffled. She moved to release herself and he let her go. She said, "You're going to help the — Gentiles — make war against us?"

"I can't believe it will come to that!" he insisted. "MacLeod says the purpose of the army is to keep peace while this trouble between the government and the Church is straightened out. You've seen how tense things are. The military will be protection for both Saints and Gentiles. They'll prevent any more outbreaks like the one we got into today, with that wagon train."

She shook her head. "No, Steve. Orson is right! They hate us! If you'd gone through what we have — I was only four when they drove us out of Missouri. In Illinois they murdered our leaders and sent us into the wilderness. Now they want to come and take away everything we've managed to build, in ten years of peace and isolation. That's what it means!"

Corey looked at her, trying to find the words to say. She had turned from him with her head averted, so that he could see only the smooth curve of her cheek. He wanted to take her in his arms again, but dared not try.

"I'm sorry," he said finally, lamely. "I can see how you feel, but I'm sure you're wrong! And in any event, for my own part I have no choice. This is a way I can repay, in some measure, the debt I owe Martin Wilcox, and it's a chance that may never come again. He needs help, desperately, if he's to get back his losses through these army contracts and set his freighting business on its feet. He can't afford to pay the wages any other man would ask to do the job. And after all, my turning him down wouldn't stop the army from coming! Surely you see I can't refuse him!"

He thought she was not going to answer. Still not looking at him, she said at last, "I suppose so. It's just that —" Her voice broke; she turned and moved quickly toward the hall doorway. She paused there with a hand upon the doorframe.

"Good-by, Steve."

He called her name but she was gone, and he heard only the whisper of her footsteps hurrying along the hall, and the closing of a door.

He became aware, slowly, of hands knotted until the nails bit into his palms. He forced the tension from him, and went out onto the porch, where Andrew Mac-Leod stood teetering at the edge of the steps, hands clasped behind him, pipeglow warming the seamed outline of his face.

"Did ye talk sense to her, lad? Or would she hear nowt of it?"

Corey's answer was grim. "I know how she feels, of course. I'm trying not to blame her for not understanding what I have to do."

"Then ye'll take the Wilcox job? Ye'll help haul supplies for the army that's marching against her people?"

The younger man shrugged heavily. "Each man has his loyalties. After all, it's my government — and my oldest friend. I've got no other choice. Surely you know that?"

"Aye."

"Then say good-by for me, tomorrow. It's no good my seeing her again. I'll be heading east, with a pack horse and the Mormon mail; and I'll be leaving early."

The old Scot nodded and offered a strong, firm hand. "Good luck to ye, lad. And keep your faith! Even in times like these, things work out."

# 3

When he first noticed the smoke it had not yet ceased billowing, black and ugly, from some point across the slightly rolling hills. The cloud it left hanging in a windless sky was enough to indicate that something of size had burned, at least a building, perhaps more than one.

It was an ominous sign; for this was Kansas Territory, and though Corey had been away he knew that the clouds of war threatening a nation divided by the slavery issue had long since broken, here, in full storm. And, guessing what the dark stain in the sky signified, he changed his course and swung in that direction across the rolling, wooded land.

He was shocked but not at all surprised to find it was a small farm that had been put to the torch, the two-room log house, the barn, a few outbuildings. A pair of bodies lay in their own blood, one before the house and another by the smoldering barn. A farmer and his grown son, they must have gone down fighting, but their weapons were missing; so was the livestock from the broken pole pen. The raiders had killed and looted before they burned. They could have been Southern sympathizers, or abolitionists of the stripe of the fanatic John Brown, or, more likely, the outlaws who rode the Territory and struck anywhere that promised loot.

Only one service remained to be done for the murdered men. With the aid of a broken-handled spade he found in the smoldering heap of charred timbers, Steve Corey buried them in the shade of scrub willows, in a dry wash where the ground was less difficult to work, and set up a board to mark the place, driving it in with blows of the spadebit. Afterward he straightened, sleeving sweat from his forehead, and glanced about. His horses were gone.

He stared, not believing, for he had heard no sound. Tied together as they were, the animals might have strayed off through the trees, but the grass was good here and he greatly doubted it. His doubt turned into cold certainty when, walking toward the place where he had left them, he saw a toeprint pressed into the loam — the mark of a boot that was not his.

Someone had crept up on him as he

worked and sneaked the horses away, whatever sounds they made covered by the noise of his digging. More than likely it was one of the raiders, hanging around afterward and going into hiding when he saw a horseman coming. The bags with their stenciling, "U.S. Mail," would have proved a great temptation.

Steve Corey swore savagely, and started to fling the broken spade from him. But then he remembered that he had unstrapped his pistol belt and hung it on the saddle for greater comfort in digging; he was unarmed. The spade, with its few inches of splintered handle, was all the weapon he had. His hand tightened about it and he started forward.

The grasses were still uncurling where the shod hoofs of the stolen horses had pressed them down. Working through the thick growth in the sheltered draw, Corey listened for every sound, expecting at any minute to hear a quick break of hoof-beats as the thief hit saddle and made off with his prize. Instead, the first warning was a crackling in brush close at hand and a little behind him. He whirled, instinctively dropping to one knee. From the tail of his eye he saw the figure lunging at him, caught the flash of a knife blade. Then, with a grunt of breath, the weight of his attacker fell upon him.

But Steve's forward move had spoiled the other's calculations. He overshot his mark; the plunging blade missed its target in Corey's unprotected shoulders. It was his bent knees that struck his victim in the back, and they both went down in a heavy tumble, Corey underneath. Kicking free of the weight that pinned him, Corey rolled and came scrambling to his knees.

The other man was but little slower; he had a wiry litheness about him, and as Corey poised with one hand against the ground, getting back his breath, the knife wielder sprang to his feet and whirled at a crouch, hunting for him. Corey saw a shine of rusty beard stubbling scarred jowls, and a matting of hair of the same dull red color. Sharp, pale eyes met his.

Then the wiry figure leaped and the wicked blade swept up, in an arc that could disembowel an enemy if the point struck home. Corey had never moved faster. On his feet now, he pivoted away from the sweep of the knife, and the broken spade in his hand swung sharply. The improvised weapon took his opponent, flat and hard, on the side of his head with all of Corey's weight behind it. It stopped the man, stun-

45

ning him. And moving in, Corey dropped him with a solid blow of his fist.

He lay with eyes closed; the bearded jaw lolled slightly open. Breathing hard, Corey leaned and lifted a gun from the man's holster, tossed it away into the brush. After that he retrieved the bowie knife which the other had dropped; he shuddered a little at its sharp-honed, ugly efficiency, and was glad to send it after the gun.

Nearby, Steve found his horses and his gun; the mailbags were still intact. He supposed the man must have a horse hidden somewhere, but did not bother looking for it; he strapped the holster in place and then, leading his own animals, went back down into the draw. He dropped the reins and squatted on his ankles beside the man he had felled.

As he wondered what to do with him, Corey made a gingerly search of the filthy clothing. The pocket of the buckskin shirt yielded nothing except a linty slab of chewing tobacco. He tried the pants, with scarcely better luck, until his searching fingers encountered a wad of paper and, bringing it out, he saw that what he held was a handful of greenbacks which the man had stuffed carelessly into his pocket. Among the bills was a crumpled piece of paper; he smoothed this out, and felt a cold tightening deep inside.

It was a pay voucher on the firm of Wilcox & Baggett. It bore the chief clerk's signature, and was drawn in the name of Bill Reno.

He was staring at it as the man beside him groaned and stirred with returning consciousness. The pale eyes wavered open, came slowly to a focus on Corey's face. They filled with rage. Fully conscious now, the man pushed to a sitting position and at the same moment caught sight of the greenbacks in Corey's hands. He slapped a palm against his empty pocket and cried out, hoarsely.

"Gimme my money!"

Corey's fingers tightened on the bills. "Bill Reno!" he said. "Since when has Martin Wilcox been hiring cutthroats like you?"

The eyes glittered. "Well, you see my name on that pay voucher."

Corey nodded. "Sure. I've heard of you, Reno! You've got a reputation that smells from here to Santa Fe. But I didn't know you'd turned border raider!"

"What?" Reno took his meaning slowly. Then, understanding, he began to stammer wildly. "Look, mister! I had nothin' to do with that. I was on an errand for my boss and I seen the smoke. I only get here a minute or two before you. I don't have to mix in this kind of thing!"

The voucher, and the size of Reno's pay, made it all sound like truth. Yet even with the evidence in front of him, Corey could not bring himself to believe it. "Your boss?" he echoed, and shook his head. "You're lying! I've heard Martin Wilcox say what he thought of you!"

"Wilcox ain't doin' the hirin'," answered Reno, triumphantly. "He's got a partner now — name of Baggett."

"And it was *Baggett* signed you on?"

All at once, this did make sense. Formless suspicions had hardened into shape; he knew then that he was none too soon in coming to learn for himself exactly what sort of a man this partner of Wilcox's really was.

"Maybe Baggett hired you," Corey said. "But you're not hired any longer. You can forget it!"

"Who says so?" The whole left side of Reno's face was beginning to swell, now, and change color. Where the spade had hit him, there was a tracery of blood through the rusty stubble of beard. It gave his ugly face a sinister cast. "Just who the hell do you think you are?"

Steve told him, and from the reaction knew that Bill Reno had heard the name. But the man said nothing, merely glowering, and Steve went on in the same cold tone.

"For an attempt on the United States mail, there's plenty I could do to you — but, you being on his payroll, that would throw Martin Wilcox in a bad light. So I'm going to have to let you go; only, don't push your luck too hard, Reno! If you know what's good for you, you won't let me set eyes on you in Leavenworth. Am I talking plain enough?"

The bearded mouth twisted. "You think I'm scared of you?"

Not bothering to answer, Steve pushed to his feet. As he started to turn away Bill Reno cried out suddenly; the bluster had turned to a whine: "You ain't gonna keep my money?"

Deliberately Steve singled out the pay voucher and then, with a contemptuous gesture, flung the crumpled handful of bills at Reno. They struck the man in the face, and fluttered about him to the ground. And, turning his back, Steve Corey got the stirrup and swung into the saddle. A kick sent his tired sorrel up the bank, with the pack horse trailing.

A keen impatience was eating at him now.

Swivel chair creaking faintly, York Baggett sat and rocked slowly, long legs stretched in front of him and head thrust forward to read the letter in his hands. As he skimmed the crabbed writing his black brow drew into a scowl. He cursed, and tossed the letter from him — then looked about, quickly anxious lest someone might have heard.

But he was alone in the freight-line office; even the high stool before the bookkeeper's ledger-laden desk was empty. Relaxing, he gave himself again to contemplation of what he had just read, long fingers knotting and kneading. He straightened suddenly and was reaching for pen and ink, when the distant sound of a packet's whistle blowing for a landing drifted through the window.

Springing to his feet he strode through the gate in the railing partition to the office door. From here he had a wide view of the river shining below, the busy wharf, and the streets leading down to it. He stood looking upon this scene, a tall man dressed with careful exactness despite the Kansas heat, his face under its receding dark hair-line perhaps too bony for real handsome-ness, yet with a certain brooding distinction.

The sights and sounds of Leavenworth landing — the scramble of soldiers and colored roustabouts to get cargo unloaded from a pair of stern-wheelers at the wharf, the voices of wagonmen cursing their teams — these combined with the eternal livestock smell of the freight yard to edge York Baggett's expression with distaste. The boat now warping in with bell ajangle and passengers lining the deck was not the freight packet he was expecting. He swung about, wearing a scowl that his surprisingly full lips turned almost into a pout.

He looked around the office. It reflected the vicissitudes of fortune that had claimed this freighting firm, over the years. The furnishings — the desks and files, the chairs with their padded leather cushions — had been elegant when new, but the leather was cracked and the mahogany chipped and scaled; it had all long since needed replacing, and Baggett made a mental note that as soon as he had a free hand it would be junked.

But just now his thoughts were full of the letter; he returned to his desk and, adjusting the tails of his steelpen coat, seated himself and took pen and paper to answer it. From the envelope he got the address of a Washington hotel, and proceeded with his heading:

My Dear Judge Amberson:
    I have read yours of the 11th inst. with some feeling of anxiety, especially the sentences wherein you suggest the possibility of resigning your commission. Believe me, this would be a very grave error. In the first place . . .

He paused to dip his pen; the scratch of the nib on paper was the only sound in the quiet room.

. . . such action would be interpreted by Brigham Young's crowd as a victory, and a sign of weakness. We must not strengthen their hands by seeming to give them exactly what they have wanted from the beginning — your removal from the federal bench of Utah Territory.
    Even more important, in my view, the present moment is one when we most need your continued help. I can of course sympathize with your feelings at

having the President pass your application over and name Alfred Cumming to be the new governor of Utah. However, I know this Cumming and in my opinion it will take every sort of prodding to force him to deal with the Mormon rebels as they deserve.

Let me point out that by retaining your judgeship you can not only give valuable aid in this, but — as I more than half predict — should Cumming prove incompetent for his post, you will be in a position to make the most of the situation that would then arise. I don't think I need elaborate.

Baggett read as much as he had written, and his lips quirked scornfully. Yes, even an ambitious fathead like Evan Amberson should be able to round in the details! And his blind need for revenge on the people who had caused his disgrace could play neatly into the hands of a far-sighted man who knew how to take advantage of it.

The next paragraph was shaping itself in his head when the sound of voices and footsteps approaching made Baggett lay aside his pen and slide the half-written letter out of sight. He had just risen as the door opened, and the three entered.

"Well! Good afternoon!"

Martin Wilcox he tabbed as a rather stupid man who had ridden the wave of the Santa Fe trade to a fortune, only to lose it through poor business sense. But Wilcox's daughter Barbara was a different matter; and she had never looked prettier, in flounces and crinolines and a bonnet tied beneath her chin with a wide blue ribbon that just matched her eyes. She was flushed and smiling, and for a moment York Baggett imagined that this was at sight of him; but as he came forward around the desk to greet her he quickly realized his mistake.

He halted, glancing at the man who had entered last and was now closing the door behind him. "Steve," Martin Wilcox said with his habitual slow dignity, "this is York Baggett, my new partner. York, you've heard me speak of Steve Corey."

"Of course." They shook hands, across the railing partition. The stranger's grip was a strong one — a challenge that Baggett met with a certain vanity in the strength of his own dry, nervous fingers. He had the impression that this Steve Corey was deliberately taking his measure, and he read dislike in the look of the brown, straight-shouldered man. "I'm delighted," he said.

Corey didn't answer. He held open the gate, and Barbara passed through ahead of him. Baggett brought a comfortable chair for her, and Wilcox got one for himself. But Corey, though he looked bone-tired and his clothing held the stain of trail dust, preferred to remain standing, leaning against the railing, arms folded and one worn boot hitched across the other.

Martin Wilcox settled himself comfortably, and said by way of preliminary, "Steve's a good man, York. I've known him a long time; he's worked for me in pretty nearly every capacity, and you can take my word for it, he's capable."

"I never questioned that." Re-seated at his desk, Baggett reached a cigar from the box in front of him. "You've explained matters to him?"

The graying, leonine head bobbed quickly. "We've been discussing it ever since he reached town, an hour ago."

"Good!" Baggett swung his look to the other man. "You know, then, that our business with the Army of Utah is a big proposition. The lion's share of the freight contracts have gone to the firm of Majors & Russell. However, being a supply contractor

I was able to close some deals with the War Department by guaranteeing to make delivery myself. And that's where Martin Wilcox enters the picture, since I don't have the equipment or the experience to do this freighting job."

He paused. Corey had said nothing, yet somehow the weight of his glance gave Baggett the feeling of a witness under cross-examination. His partner took up the story.

"We're allowed a good margin of profit," Martin Wilcox said, "but it does mean a large initial outlay — new wagons and livestock to buy, a secondary shipping point to be established at a more convenient location. So, the way it works out, York will operate from this headquarters, while I locate our new branch upriver. And, York," he added, "it seems to me there are any number of ways a man like Steve Corey can be valuable to us."

"Oh, very true," Baggett agreed quickly, toying with the unlighted cigar. "As it happens, I have a good skeleton crew here — a yard boss and wagonmasters I'm perfectly confident in. I'd say, then, it's a question of what's needed up at Nebraska City."

Steve Corey looked from one to the other. "Nebraska City? Don't think I've heard of it."

Wilcox explained. "It's a little town, but a good natural river landing. It's an open secret that Alex Majors plans to move his base of operations there, and what's good enough for Majors ought to suit us! I've already looked the place over, and leased ground for a freight yard and warehouse. Oh, I told you, Steve, things are breaking fast!"

"Apparently!"

"You saw for yourself how the whole frontier is boiling with this Mormon trouble. There was that emigrant outfit you told me about — what was the captain's name? Fancher?" As Corey nodded, Wilcox turned to explain to his partner: "A California train, heading through Salt Lake Valley. Steve ran into them at Fort Laramie and heard some hard talk about stringing up Brigham Young. Some Mormons who happened to hear it would have started a fight right there if Steve hadn't broken it up."

"You don't say so!" Baggett shook his head. "Well, there's no doubt in my mind those Mormons have been asking for trouble —"

"That's a matter of opinion!" Corey said quickly.

Then Barbara Wilcox spoke up, her face

troubled. "Dad, Steve's showed us how he feels about all this. Maybe it's not fair of us to ask him to get involved."

"You aren't suggesting Steve Corey isn't loyal to his country?" her father exclaimed, and answered his own question. "Of course that isn't what you meant. And I agree. I wouldn't want to push you into anything, Steve. Why not think it over? Take a day or two, then let us know how you decide."

There was a moment's stillness, broken by the pop of a sulphur as York Baggett put it to the cigar he had chosen. Dragging at it, he peered through the smoke at the dark face of the man who leaned, arms still folded, against the partition railing. Then Corey was speaking, in that same quiet voice, his eyes pinned on Baggett's.

"I've already decided. I'll take the job, but I'd rather define the terms myself. The pay doesn't matter. Just put me down as a field man, to work here or in Nebraska City or on the trails — any place I'm needed. I know all that country west; I know the sort of problems we'll face. I can serve you best if you give me a free hand."

York Baggett scowled. He lowered the cigar, staring at this man. Groping for arguments, he had to wet his lips before he could speak. "Really, I don't —"

He got no further. For Martin Wilcox was on his feet, pumping Corey's hand and exclaiming, "Thank you, my boy! I couldn't have asked anything better! Now at last I'm sure I haven't bit off a job too big for me!"

And Bobby Wilcox, reaching, had Corey's other hand in both of hers and she sat clutching it like that, pretty face beaming her pleasure. Baggett knew then that arguments would be useless; and when he found Steve Corey's gaze resting on him again, burning into him like a slow acid, he forced a smile and a curt nod of agreement.

Minutes later he was alone again, glaring in fury at the closed door. He picked up the cigar and carried it to his lips, then in a savage gesture flung it into the spittoon beside his high-buttoned, polished shoe.

He brought out the half-finished letter from his desk but, changing his mind, thrust it away again. For this talk had suddenly put a fresh thought into his head. Toying with this, he reached for pad and pencil and began to trace a name, over and over, until the letters were heavy and black. The name was "FANCHER." He looked at it for long minutes, then suddenly ripped off the sheet, crumpled it in strong, lean fingers and tossed it into a wastebasket.

After that he was on his feet, taking a black, narrow-brimmed hat from the top of a file cabinet. The office door closed silently behind him.

# 4

Steve Corey walked home with Barbara Wilcox, through black pools of shade that dusty trees laid against the white light of afternoon. The dry sidewalk plankings echoed their unhurried footsteps. Her hand resting lightly on his arm, her full skirts swaying against his dusty boots, she twirled a frilly parasol and let her bright chatter run on. Fortunately he did not have to answer; dark and troubling thoughts, born of that talk in the freight-line office, held him and were reflected in the hard line of his mouth.

He was surprised out of this mood when Bobby shook his elbow and exclaimed, "You aren't even listening to me! You look mad about something, Steve."

"Sorry!" A smile broke across his face. "You were saying — ?"

"Just that it's like old times, having you back with us."

"What would you know about the old times?" They had paused in their walking, and still smiling he reached a thumb to draw down her lower lip, revealing the even, pearly teeth.

"Just what do you think you're doing?"

"When I first knew you, Bobby, you had a gap there in front."

She pushed his hand away. "Oh, I never!"

"That was ten years ago," he reminded her. "You weren't so big."

"You think I'm still a child," she said, and added archly, "Well, I'm not. I'm quite grown up!" She swung away from him. He laughed and caught her arm.

"I never said you weren't. You're a real lady, and a lovely one. There, is that better?"

For once she was taken without a word to say. But she let Corey fall in step beside her again, and he knew he was forgiven.

With the approach of sunset, a breeze had come up and was swaying the heads of the catalpa trees as they halted beside the picket fence surrounding Martin Wilcox's big frame house. Her hand upon the gate, Barbara shook her head with a little sigh. "I'll be sorry to leave this place."

"Leave? You're going to Nebraska City with your father?"

"Why, of course. He needs me to take care of him!"

The thought of this slip of a girl protecting bluff Martin Wilcox tempted Corey to smile, but he carefully refrained. She told him, "You're staying to dinner, you know."

"Oh, I am?"

"Now, don't argue!" The girl took his arm, drawing him with her along the walk to the house. "It's all arranged. You forget how long it's been since you sat at our table."

He gave in. It was never any use trying to keep Bobby Wilcox from having her own way.

They ate by the light of candles in beaten bronze holders. The soft gleam fell on the silver table service and the carved sideboard that were among the few good pieces Martin Wilcox had managed to hold onto in the years since the decline of his fortunes. There was an old colored woman to serve them; and Bobby looked very much the hostess in a charming, low-cut gown above which her young shoulders and throat shone like ivory. And her chatter set the tone of the meal.

Corey was tired, not in a mood for conversation. Afterward, the girl excused herself and the two men sat over their coffee and cigars. As he got his smoke going and dropped the twisted sulphur stick into his saucer, the older man looked at his guest through a ribbon of smoke and spoke, earnestly.

"I can't put into words just how grateful I am, Steve. If you had turned me down, this job could not have been done — time as limited as it is."

Corey passed off the thanks. "When do you leave for Nebraska City?"

"Right away, now you're here to take over. You can well imagine I'll have to throw a terrific amount of the burden on you. There's equipment and stock to buy, competent crews to be screened and hired. . . ."

"I'll do my best. But I suppose you realize what's going to happen, as soon as word gets out we're in the market and bidding against Majors & Russell? Prices will jump fifty percent overnight, and wages will be out of sight. There just aren't enough wagons and trained bullwackers available for an operation of this size. I only hope you can stand the tariff!"

"My credit's in pretty good shape."

"How about this partner of yours? Are you getting any cut on these supply contracts, in addition to the freighting itself?"

Wilcox frowned slightly. "After all, the

nature of our partnership —"

"I see." Corey twisted his cigar between his fingers, studying the glowing end. What he saw was that York Baggett was putting up nothing, risking nothing in this enterprise. If it failed, only Wilcox stood to lose the tremendous investment he was making. "Just how well do you know him, Martin?" he asked. "Know anything of his past dealings with the army?"

"You're hinting at something!" exclaimed Wilcox, sharply. "I don't understand you, Steve! This is my one hope of getting back what I've lost, and founding a sure basis for Bobby's future. Yours too, my boy, if you'll stay with me."

It was somehow pathetic — Martin's need to believe in this opportunity, and in the man who had made it possible. Seeing the need reflected in his old friend's troubled eyes, Steve Corey knew his questions were fruitless and was sorry for having put them. He said, "Thanks, Martin. We'll see. And forget the questions — I was only asking." He pushed back his chair. "It's a big job ahead of us; I'll get on it first thing in the morning."

"Good boy!" Wilcox immediately lost his reserve and became smiling again as he saw that there was to be no more probing.

He said as they both rose, "Shall we go see what Bobby's doing?"

A breath of coolness had come with the falling of darkness. When Steve Corey stepped out again upon the deep veranda, calling back his good nights, lamplight made its pattern in the windows of the town and a round yellow moon hung in the branches of the catalpas.

Bobby had come out with him and they stood together a moment, enjoying the evening. Moonglow laid its sheen on the girl's hair, parted in the middle and combed back in a cascade of ash-blond curls. A wisp of shawl lay against her throat, above the charming swell of her young figure in the low-cut gown.

"Good night, Bobby," Steve said, squeezing her hand.

"If you don't let Dad know," she told him, "you may kiss me."

As well refuse a friendly kitten that asks for a caress. Smiling, he crooked a forefinger beneath her chin to lift it, and bent to meet her lips. They were as soft as a flower, her kiss simple and untutored; he heard her catch her breath and when he straightened, her eyes were closed and her lips a little parted. Corey frowned, and dropped his hand. Somehow the effect on him had not been quite as casual and innocent as he had meant it to be.

He said again, a little roughly, "Good night." And swinging away, he dropped down the steps and along the pathway to the gate. When he glanced back, she was still standing, unmoving and softly white, against the shadows of the veranda.

Later, in his hotel room, Steve Corey sat in the dark by an open window, where the night brought him scents of scorched earth mingled with the dark, damp odors of the river. He was incredibly tired, yet his mind turned restlessly under the stimulus of the day's events, and the pull of conflicting loyalties.

These were strong ties that had renewed their hold on him, yet no stronger than those that drew his thoughts across the miles to other friends — and to the girl he loved. The problems of Martin Wilcox, and his suspicious dislike of York Baggett were forgotten in this longing. He groaned and, rising, went to the table and lit the lamp. He took pencil and paper and seated himself to write, in his strong, bold hand, the words, "My Darling." But then the blank page stared at him mockingly.

His emotions and thoughts were too

confused, too dulled with fatigue. After the things that had been said that last night, in the sutler's living room at Laramie, no words seemed good enough to have any effect.

He crumpled the paper, tossed it from him.

# 5

Though he rose early, the town was already awake and boiling with activity. He ate in the hotel dining room, where he listened to the talk around him while he leafed quickly through the Kansas City *Journal of Commerce*, bringing himself up to date on the events of this other world he had returned to. The paper was full of the excitement over the Mormon dispute, and he studied the editorials carefully, his eyes glinting with anger.

A fat man across the table from him, who also had a paper, said, "Here's the letter Judge Amberson wrote to the President, after the Mormons kicked him out of office."

"I was reading it," said Corey, angrily. "Nothing but lies!"

His outburst brought him a curious glance. "You claim to know the facts?"

"Some." Belatedly Corey remembered that it would be best to watch his tongue, where the temper was as predominantly anti-Mormon as on the Missouri border. "I spent some months out there. I don't know how Amberson got his appointment but I will say I never saw any man less fit for office. I've watched him try to hold court when he was so fuddled with booze he could hardly sit straight on the bench. If you knew the Saints, you'd realize what an insult it was, having a thing like that set over them to administer the law!"

The man looked entirely dubious. "Seems to me I'd take a federal judge's word, against some filthy polygamist's. Says right here that Brigham Young had the nerve to go and burn all the federal books and court documents."

"More lies!"

The fat man shrugged and folded his paper. "That's destroyin' gover'ment property," he said, doggedly. "If there's truth in it, them Mormons had ought to be punished. And," he added, rising and stabbing Corey with a look, "a man that makes careless talk at a time like this, with what looks like a war shaping up — he could get himself in trouble. Bad trouble!"

Corey's jaw clamped hard. After the other had left the table he sat for a time thinking about what had been said, drawing his lesson and his warning from it. He could do neither himself nor Martin Wilcox any good by letting himself be branded as a Mormon sympathizer. Despite any personal feelings, his first duty was to his country and to this friend who had the promise of his help.

He took his sorrel from the hotel stable and rode over to the Wilcox house, a trifle uneasy over a meeting with Barbara after last evening. But when he dismounted at the gate, a black single-seated buggy and bay were waiting and Martin Wilcox came out of the house with a jaunty step, nodding and smiling a greeting to Corey. "I suppose you're here to see Bobby, but I'm going to ask you to wait awhile. I was just starting out for a look at operations. Care to come along?"

"Sure." Steve tied his sorrel to the buggy and got in beside his employer, as the older man took the reins in hands that were tough and strong and blotched with freckles — hands that had worked a bull whip under the hot sun of the trail to Santa Fe before Steve Corey was born. Rolling through the dusty streets of Leavenworth, Steve had a closer look at him and saw telltale signs of aging, signs that a casual glance might have missed.

There was a network of fine wrinkles about the eyes and cheeks, a sagging of the flesh of the throat, a rounding of the shoulders as though that massive head was becoming a bit too heavy for them now. There was slowness in his movements, too, that hadn't been there before. But Martin Wilcox still retained most of his vigor, and Steve suspected it was the hardships and disappointments of these recent years, and not the mere passing of time, that had been able to tell upon that fabulous spirit and zest for life.

As they came to the edge of town Wilcox pointed out, with his whip, freight yards that completely dwarfed his own modest layout. "Majors & Russell," he explained. "Now, there's a real freighting firm; compared to them, we're nothing but small fry! They're getting all the lion's share of the army's freight to Utah. It was only by promising earlier delivery than Majors was willing to guarantee, that York managed to land the contracts supplying the advance column of the Utah Expedition."

This was news to Corey, and it explained a good many things. "So *you've* got to make that promise good? A big order to have dumped in your lap!"

"True enough. But it's a wonderful opportunity, and I was glad enough for the chance at it, on any terms. So far I've had luck digging up the wagons and stock we need, and the first trains are scheduled to roll by the end of the week. But these yards will be swamped once supplies really start pouring off the boats — that's why we've got to have our new ones at Nebraska City in operation, as fast as we can manage."

Corey looked at his friend closely. "Stretching it kind of thin, maybe?"

"I hardly think so. An army contract is the same as money in the bank."

"But suppose something should happen to the trains? It's midsummer already; the rate the campaign's getting under way, it could be autumn before it actually takes the field."

It was Martin Wilcox's turn to appear troubled; the warning must have struck upon a thought that had not occurred to him. He tried to voice a confidence that perhaps he didn't entirely feel. "They surely wouldn't order a winter campaign — not in the mountains!"

"Who knows what the army will do? Just remember: Where those troops are sent, your supply trains will have to go right along with them. And they'll be facing an enemy that knows the country thoroughly."

Martin said, slowly, "You really think,

then, the Mormons will fight?"

"No question of it!"

The two were quiet after that, sobered both by their talk and by the sight that met them as the town fell back and they came upon the rolling prairie between town and fort.

It was an amazing panorama, enough to stir the blood of any freighter — the toiling men, the row on row of canvas-topped wagons capable of loading six thousand pounds each, the piles of yokes and spare wagon tongues and ironwork, the pens where heavy oxen kept up a babel of lowing. Dust drifted everywhere, turned saffron under the high, beating sun. There was such an air of purposeful activity, of work being done under terrific pressures, that Steve Corey grew conscious of the heightening of his pulses despite his dark reservations concerning the purpose of it all.

Wilcox pulled up at a safe distance so they could watch sweating teamsters laboring with the untamed oxen, breaking them to the yoke with rough-and-ready methods. When these wagons took the trail for Utah, only the lead teams for the most part would be really tame and trained to their work; the bulk of the half-wild beasts would be yoked by main force and hooked into their places on the poles. They would be tame enough when the long haul was finished.

Yonder, lines of empty wagons raised dust along the roads to the fort for loading at the quartermaster's warehouse; others rumbled up from the wharf where troops on fatigue duty were emptying the holds of river packets. "We'll be on the road on time," Wilcox declared again, pride in his voice over what had been accomplished.

Steve was watching a big, black-headed shape of a man who strode about bellowing orders, which the toiling men were quick to obey. There was something familiar about the solid figure, the long legs and the barrel-like torso in a sweaty shirt with sleeves whacked off near the shoulder to reveal heavily muscled arms. "Who's the big gun?" Steve asked, pointing. "Jud Noonan, isn't it?"

"Baggett hired him to act as yard boss." Wilcox frowned at the look on Corey's face. "You don't approve?"

Corey shrugged. "I'd hate to be working under him. But I guess I don't really know anything against him."

"He's hard, I'll grant, but it takes an extra toughness to do a job like this, in the time we're allowed. And I'll have to say that Noonan is doing it."

"Glad to hear it," Steve said, but his voice held a trace of dryness.

Wilcox told him, "Well, I've got work waiting at the office — a table of equipment we need for the Nebraska City yard. It will take another hour or two before it's ready to show you. Shall we turn back?"

"You go ahead. I'll be in later to look at the papers; right now I think I'll stick around and watch this awhile."

"Of course."

Steve stepped down from the buggy and freed his sorrel's reins. When his employer had started back toward the freight-yard office, the light vehicle raising its own small plume of tawny dust, he mounted and rode on alone. He kept out of the way, on the fringe of activity, while he observed it with professional interest.

And he discovered himself searching the sweaty faces, looking for one in particular — a scarred, red-bearded face, narrow ugliness in the pale blue eyes. But he saw no sign of Bill Reno. Maybe the knife-thrower had actually taken his warning.

He reined in to watch a man at work on one of the big wagons, giving it a last checkup. The man worked smoothly but

76

thoroughly, and Corey noted with approval the care with which every likely trouble spot received its particular attention. Now he was using a lift-jack to raise one of the sixteen-spoke rear wheels. He had a gunnysack with which he wrapped the heavy lock chain, to prevent its doing damage to the spokes and felly; he checked the tightness of the heavy four-inch metal tire, and then used his tools to pull the linch-pin that held the wheel in place.

At that particular moment, Jud Noonan came along the line of wagons, and he stopped briefly to flick a hurried glance over the work that was being done. "That wagon's all right," he pronounced, shortly. "You can leave it."

Not answering, the big man proceeded to work the wheel off the iron skein of the axle, lift it down to lean against the wagonbox. Corey saw Noonan's head jerk, angrily. "You understand English? I said the rig's all right. We ain't got time to fool around."

Slowly, the man turned. He was a big fellow, with the appearance of a Swede, and an unruffled manner, with which he met the other's angry stare. He jerked a thumb at the exposed axle end. "Look at the dirt that's worked in there, Mr.

Noonan. And a thousand dry miles to cover. Takes a lot of greasin' to keep 'em in shape." And he stepped to fetch the tarbucket from its hook beneath the rear axle.

With a look of fury, Noonan took him by the shoulder, yanked him around. "When you work for me, damn you, you follow orders!"

"No, sir. I do the job proper, or I —"

Noonan hit him, a staggering blow. Before the Swede could recover, a gun had slid into the hand of the yard boss to halt him in his tracks. "Go draw your pay!" Noonan said. "You're through."

Flushed from the blow, the Swede looked at Jud Noonan. His shoulders hunched, and Steve Corey saw his competent hands work a little, but there was no arguing with a drawn weapon. Without a word, the man turned his back and started to walk stolidly away.

"Just a minute," said Corey.

He had watched and listened without moving and apparently without drawing notice; now, however, the Swede halted and Jud Noonan's glance swung toward him, as Steve deliberately lifted a boot from stirrup and stepped down. To the yellow-haired man he said, "I'll be glad to hire you, friend. At the same wages."

The man gave him a slow and curious look. "What outfit?"

"This one, the Nebraska City branch. I'm signing crews for Martin Wilcox."

He saw the man's slow mind work over the matter, and then the Swede nodded. "Suits me. I worked for Mr. Wilcox before this tough crowd took charge — and I don't think I care much for Leavenworth, any more."

"What's your name?"

"Jorgesen. Ole Jorgesen."

"I'm Steve Corey." He offered his hand and the Swede shook with him. After that, Jorgesen was gone, plodding away through the dust and leaving the wagon with its rear axle jacked up and the wheel leaning where he had set it against the box. Steve watched him go, turning then to find Jud Noonan's stare heavy upon him, a belated recognition in the man's scowling eyes. Deliberately Noonan shoved his cap-and-ball Navy back into its holster.

"It's really Steve Corey, ain't it? The Mormon lover."

"Better watch your tongue, Jud!"

"Why?" The man's lips took on an open sneer. "Word gets around: it's common knowledge where you been spending the past year. Old Brigham's right-hand man, they say!"

"It was a business proposition," Corey told him. "And I think you know it. The Saints needed a mail express route laid out; they paid me to do the job."

"I just bet they did!" There was a mean devil of reckless spite in Noonan. He pitched his voice louder. "Don't reckon I'd care for the stink of Mormon money!" he declared, scornfully. "But then, that maybe wasn't what they paid you off with — not as long as they got more of them slutty women than they know what to —"

Too late, he moved to scoop out the gun he had slid into its holster. Steve was on him, and the hard, whipping edge of his left wrist struck Noonan's gun-hand, knocked the gun spinning from his fingers. Noonan swore and batted out with a left fist. Steve jerked away and it grazed his cheek, struck his shoulder with enough weight to break his stride.

Noonan was not a small man, and his tremendous arms carried hard muscle. But Corey had not bossed wagon trains to Santa Fe and California without learning to hold his own in the style of fighting that was apt to end in a stomped face or a gouged eye. Regaining his balance, he

80

drove his own right fist squarely into the foreman's face. Noonan grunted in pain and fell back against the wagon, his shoulders striking the big wheel Jorgesen had propped there; before he could brace himself Corey slugged him in the belly and, when he started to double, on the side of his shaggy head. The propped wheel pivoted under the man's weight, and Noonan went down heavily into the dirt beneath the jacked-up wagon.

"Your mouth is too damned big," Corey said. Noonan only lay in the dust, conscious but groggy and winded. Looking at him, and flexing numbed and aching fingers, Corey felt a reaction and he knew he would probably regret letting his anger take control.

He turned and walked back to his horse, but he did not mount at once. For he saw that a knot of men — five or six of the big Wilcox & Baggett teamsters — were coming toward him, across the yard. He tensed, expecting trouble, until he saw that their faces held no hostile purpose.

They stopped in front of him and one, speaking for the rest, said gruffly, "Heard you say you're hirin' for that Nebraska City yard. Need any more men?"

He understood the respect in their eyes.

81

Yet he hesitated over his answer.

"I'll pay no man a bonus for quitting his job here," he said. "But I do need teamsters. I'll match the wages any other freight company is paying."

Satisfied nods greeted this answer. The spokesman said, "That's as much as *I* need to know!"

The lot of them turned and tramped off in the direction of the distant wagon yard, in Ole Jorgesen's wake. Steve watched them go, knowing he had started trouble; but he felt that he had been pushed into it. He looked again at Jud Noonan, and saw the man sitting up and staunching a bloody nose against a hairy arm.

He swung himself into the saddle.

Walking into the freight-yard office a half hour later, he saw that trouble had preceded him. Jud Noonan, nose swollen and the whole side of his cheek shaping into a livid bruise, was at the railing talking angrily with York Baggett; they both turned sharply as Steve closed the door behind him. A clerk stared, and at the rear of the room Martin Wilcox quickly laid down the papers he was working on and started forward, his expression worried.

Baggett's voice was severe, as he spoke without preliminaries: "Corey, will you tell

82

me exactly what you're up to? Are you trying to undermine this organization, or what?"

"A half-dozen men have already been in to draw their time," Wilcox explained quickly. "They said you hired them away from their jobs to go to Nebraska City."

"And what did you tell them?"

"To get back to work, of course," York Baggett answered, "or they were through at Wilcox & Baggett!"

Corey met his look, levelly. "Too bad," he said, "because it just means we've lost a bunch of men we could have used! I was trying to hold onto them. They'll quit, all right, and go over to Majors & Russell or some other outfit. I've seen enough this morning to convince me a lot of men have had a bellyful of the treatment they've been taking here!"

He sensed the tension that came into Baggett and his yard boss. It was Wilcox who said, "Maybe you'd better explain what you mean by that, Steve!"

"I just mean you can't rawhide a crew, senselessly, the way Jud Noonan has been doing. They'll do the work and do it right, given half a chance. But beyond a certain point they won't take it — not when work's as easy to find as it is these days!"

Jud Noonan was still smarting from the blows that had laid him out and made a spectacle of him in front of the crew. His big hands, fur-backed, curled into fists and his bruised head lowered, "So you don't like the way I run this freight yard?"

"Any law says I have to?"

Steve looked at Martin Wilcox and saw the distress in his old friend's face. "There's a fellow named Ole Jorgesen. Noonan fired him — for taking time to do an adequate job of greasing a wagon — so he's fair game for us, and no reason his name shouldn't go on the payroll for Nebraska City. He's a good man. I want him."

"Steve —" Wilcox began, anxiously; but York Baggett broke in unexpectedly and his whole manner had altered.

"It's all right, Martin," he said in a surprising tone of conciliation, that brought him Steve's stare and left Noonan helpless and without support. "An honest difference of opinion, no reason for hard feelings. We'll let it drop."

But Steve Corey was beyond compromise. "I'm not quite ready to let it drop," he said, "now that things have come to a head. It may be none of my business — but, Martin, are you satisfied having a man like Bill Reno draw wages from this outfit?"

"Bill Reno!" Wilcox's look went grave, and he turned to his partner. "York, I would certainly hope —"

Baggett, narrowly observed by Steve, said sharply, "I never heard the name!"

For answer, Corey brought out the payroll voucher he had taken from Reno, and passed it to his boss. Martin Wilcox looked at it, and his face hardened. As he lifted his head and speared York Baggett with a questioning glance, the latter touched tongue to dry lips. "Now, just a minute!" he blurted. "Is this thing turning into a cross-examination? I couldn't swear to every name that might be on our payroll, not after all the men I've screened these past weeks. What does it matter, anyway? You yourself said we need all the wagon handlers we can get, even if some we may get aren't choice!"

"That's true enough," his partner answered in a stern voice. "Just the same, we can't have the scum of the Border working for us! Being a newcomer, of course, it's understandable you mightn't know this Bill Reno's reputation." He turned to Jud Noonan, who was listening to all this with a scowl in his eyes. "Find the man and pay him off. Tell him we don't need him."

Noonan straightened. He shot an uncertain look at Baggett but got no help from that quarter. He rubbed the knuckles of a black-furred hand across his jaw, and nodded. "If I see him," he muttered. "I'll look around. But somebody told me he was in town last night, and left again."

He gave Corey a last stabbing, angry glance before he turned and tramped out of the building, taking his sweaty smell with him.

Wilcox said, "Steve, I've got those equipment tables ready to go over with you."

"All right." Having learned what he wanted, Corey was willing to let this other matter rest. He followed Wilcox through the gate in the low partition railing, coolly meeting Baggett's angry look. He had seen murder in men's eyes before; he was seeing it now.

Why, he wondered, had Baggett tried to cover with a lie his hiring of Bill Reno?

Meanwhile, there was Noonan's report that Reno had been in town, and mysteriously left again. It would be interesting to know if Reno was heeding Corey's warning to stay out of Leavenworth — or if, perhaps, he had merely been sent to run another errand. Only York Baggett could have answered that question.

It was safe to say that he would not.

# 6

As MacLeod had told him, events had a momentum of their own and a man could sometimes find himself caught up and carried relentlessly on their current like a chip on a swollen stream. So it was now with Steve Corey.

The summer passed swiftly, a summer of mounting tension, when the dusty roads saw the long blue columns of the Utah Expedition march west out of Leavenworth — foot soldiers at route step, muskets slung and banners snapping crisply — and the big Wilcox & Baggett wagon trains leaving, loaded to the bows with supplies.

Corey was on the go himself, constantly. His was a job that took him on endless missions up and down the Missouri Border: to Kansas City wagon yards, to check the specifications on an order of the huge, wooden-axled freight rigs before letting them be sent on to Nebraska City; then upriver to Weston to look at some mules; and over into Iowa where draft oxen were to be had more cheaply than in the competitive Kansas market. True to his prediction, prices and wages had nearly doubled; working within Martin Wilcox's tight resources, it took all of Corey's ingenuity and knowledge to keep expenditures from mounting out of reason.

And all the while his own inner turmoils — the worrying concern for Melissa Tyler, and his other Mormon friends — must be reserved for those few odd hours when the pressure of his tasks gave him time for thinking.

The news from the West was utterly disturbing. All negotiations between the Saints and the federal government had apparently broken down after Brigham Young's flat refusal to accept dismissal from office on the appointment of a Gentile as his successor. Brigham denied categorically all charges of destroying federal court records or tampering with the mail that passed through Salt Lake City. He had defied the legality of any armed force that might enter the Territory by declaring martial law and promising that Echo Canyon and the entrances to the Basin would be defended to the last man; and if the army broke through, he said, it would find nothing but a desert — every house and farm destroyed and the people fled into the mountains, even as far as Mexico.

He was even reported to have made a darker threat: "If the Gentiles come against me, I shall no longer promise to hold my red brother by the wrist. . . ." And this warning of Indian warfare was enough to send a shudder of dread down the very spine of the frontier. Knowing Brigham — his strong and sometimes ruthless will — Corey could read the desperation that lay behind such loud defiance.

In sweltering September weather he came for the first time to Nebraska City, aboard a sidewheeler that carried a dozen big Espenshieds for the new yards lashed to its decks. Martin Wilcox had been expecting him and before the boat was brought in to a tie-up, he had a crew and teams waiting on the dock to accept the wagons as they were unloaded, and haul them up the steep hill to the freight yard. One of the men was the Swede, Jorgesen, and he greeted Corey with a white-toothed grin and the wave of a hand. Another was a slim, good-looking youngster who seemed to be in charge of the crew; Wilcox called him over for an introduction.

"This is Ed Loman, Steve. I want you to work with him. I figure he has the makings of a wagonmaster."

"Glad to know you, Mr. Corey." Loman gave him a respectful look and a strong grip.

Corey liked his looks at once; later, as he and Wilcox walked together through the bustling, raw river town, he said so. "The boy seems capable, Martin. Where did you pick him up?"

"Why, he just came around looking for work. Turned out that he'd had a lot of experience — did shotgun freighting along with an older brother, until the Indians got the other boy's scalp. Last year he handled mules with an outfit to Santa Fe. He knows mules and oxen, and he knows the trails. Makes me think of you, a few years back — maybe that's one reason I've taken him under my wing."

Corey suspected there might be other reasons when, an hour later, he glanced from a window of Wilcox's new office and saw young Loman and Bobby Wilcox standing very close together, talking and laughing over the private excitements of youth. He didn't miss the rapt look on the girl's pretty face, or the way she tucked her hand beneath the lad's arm as they turned to stroll away.

He heard an amused and indulgent chuckle in Martin Wilcox's throat. "A handsome pair of kids!" Corey had to admit it. His own greeting from Bobby had been friendly as usual, but a shade impersonal; that kiss she had let him take, so many weeks ago on the deep veranda in Leavenworth, seemed utterly forgotten. Now he understood, and he couldn't be jealous — not when confronted by a good, clean pair of youngsters who were as well suited as those two, and apparently already deep in love.

He returned to the subject they had been discussing.

"Well, there it is, Martin — there's the picture. We've spread as thin as we'd better, I think, until we begin to collect something from the government. The stock and equipment are here or will be, as fast as they can be delivered. Our job now is to put trains together, and throw them on the trail."

Wilcox nodded in satisfaction, and slapped his desk with the flat of a hand. "You've done wonders; I don't know how you manage. Maybe it's because I'm getting old, myself, and slowing down."

He didn't look particularly old, just now. Excitement and activity had taken years from him, these last weeks. "I get regular reports from York Baggett, in Leavenworth," he went on. "Things there are proceeding on schedule, with a half-dozen trains already sent out. I've notified him we're ready to commence operations, and the first consignments of military stores for this yard should be in on the boats next week or the week after. By that time, we'll be set up to load them right into the wagons."

"Good!" Steve took his hat from the desk, twirled it between strong and restless hands. "With matters going that smoothly, there's hardly anything further I can contribute at this end. So if it's all right with you, I think I'll ride out as supercargo with the first bunch of wagons."

From the look Wilcox gave him, the man might have read something hidden in his voice. "Any particular reason?"

"Why, for one thing I want to look at the route you'll be using, west of here. I want to see how the Plains Indians are taking this business, though with all the military traffic shuttling back and forth, I imagine they're lying quiet. After that —" He lifted a shoulder. "I dunno — a hunch, maybe. But I'll feel better if I can see with my own eyes what happens to these wagons and their loads at the other end. Wouldn't want any bottlenecks developing, when they pour into Fort Laramie. One of us ought to be on the ground."

The other man considered for a long moment before he nodded agreement. "Whatever you say, Steve. As general agent, you'll have full power to act for me: collect any money, make any expenditures, sell the wagons and stock and equipment when they reach Utah if that seems advisable. Yes, you've made a very good suggestion. I'll draw up the necessary papers."

Steve Corey wondered if his old friend sensed there were stronger, personal reasons for his wanting to get back out there — why it was he felt trapped, remaining on the Missouri Border while in Utah things would be shaping to a crisis. But if Martin Wilcox guessed more than Steve was willing to tell him, he asked no questions. And for this the younger man could only thank him silently.

It was the change of the season; a little space of three weeks was long enough, at that latitude and that time of year, to kill off the final lingering heat and usher in the winter. When Steve Corey brought the first trainload of goods from Nebraska City into Laramie, summer was already a forgotten time. Low, bellying clouds shrouded the hills. October's frosts had seared the prairie to a tawny monotone and nearly stripped the branches of sparse creekbank timber. The wiry sorrel was already shaggy with its new winter coat.

Impatience rode heavily on him, making him shortspoken, and creating a distance between him and his wagon crew.

When, with the fort in sight, he left the train to ride ahead and arrange delivery, Ed Loman ventured to delay him long enough to ask a favor. Wilcox had taken advantage of Corey's presence with the train to send young Loman out as second in command, so that Corey could observe how the young man stacked up, and perhaps give Loman the benefit of his own seasoned knowledge. Ed had stacked up well indeed. He had sense, and experience, and that indefinable quality that made older men willing to take him on equal terms and accept his orders. He pulled a bulky envelope from his pocket, now, hesitantly.

"Would you drop this in a mail sack for me, Steve?"

Corey smiled as he saw the bulk of the letter, and Ed flushed a little, grinning, and embarrassed. "Finally got it finished?" Corey had watched him working on the letter, beside trail fires and noon camps, all the way across — adding a few paragraphs at a time, daily swelling the pad of penciled foolscap he carried along in his pocket together with the tintype Bobby Wilcox had given him at parting. Some time this morning he must have brought it to a close, and folded and sealed the lengthy document.

Bobby's last words to Steve when she said good-by had been a hurried, whispered injunction: "You'll watch out for him, won't you? You won't let anything happen? You've got to promise!" And he had been glad to promise it, even though he had a strong suspicion that young Loman could likely take very good care of himself.

He smiled and shook his head, refusing the package. "I wouldn't want the responsibility of maybe losing that! You keep it, kid, and mail it yourself. You'll be hitting the sutler's as soon as I do."

The boy nodded a little sheepishly. "All right." He returned the envelope to his pocket as Corey reined his sorrel about and kicked it forward.

"Keep 'em rolling," Corey told him, and with a careless salute spurted ahead over the swells of frost-browned prairie. Quickly he left behind the strung-out line of wagons, slow-moving with the heavy payloads beneath dust-streaked canvas. The buildings of the fort came into view and grew larger as he neared. His eyes, narrowing, saw the change that a few brief months had brought here.

He had known Laramie in many moods, but had never imagined it quite the way he saw it now. There were a thousand smokes, it seemed, lifting not only from adobe chimneys but from the countless mess fires scattered among a broad white spread of the army's newly adopted Sibley tents. The smoke rose lazily to mingle in a hazy stratum of dead air, forming a pallid canopy for the busy preparation of a large-scale military campaign.

Blue-clad troops were drilling in dust that rose tawny yellow, as they wheeled and maneuvered in columns of four, weaving a pattern across the crisp prairie stubble, rifles glittering aslant of shoulders, barked commands of their non-coms coming faintly across the distance. There were herds of draft oxen and army mules, and the billowing tops of rank after rank of huge freight wagons — Wilcox & Baggett rigs, all of them. Yonder, teamsters made repairs or worked with the half-broken oxen.

He crossed the Laramie at a shallow fording and swung in toward the fort. A thunderous scowl grew on him, seeing the condition of the wagon camp.

Trash littered the torn earth. Once, the sorrel's hoof struck glass and an empty whisky bottle was sent spinning and winking, to shatter on a stone. Harness lay scattered and tangled. Canvas that should have been roped taut above valuable cargoes sagged instead upon its bows, or even showed an occasional rent that had not been mended. Bronzed face gone hard, Steve Corey passed along the rows and tallied these deficiencies with a sure glance that missed no small detail.

He saw a big rear wheel canted out from its axle at a suspicious angle, and kneed the sorrel over for a closer look. He had laid a hand on the wide iron tire when the shout came:

"Hey! Damn you, get away from that!"

Turning he met Jud Noonan's startled look as the big man halted in midstride, recognizing him. Beyond, three others stood near one of the big freight wagons, watching. A couple of these were teamsters; the third lowered the demijohn that he held half-raised to his mouth. It was York Baggett.

Baggett had a boot heel cocked up on a spoke of the big wheel; he took it down now, and straightened. "Well!" he grunted in a tone of mockery. "It's friend Corey!"

Steve could not escape the unpleasant shock of surprise that went through him. He stared at Baggett, his dislike tempered by a strange feeling that Baggett had changed in the weeks since their last meeting. It was hard to put a name to this change, but it was there. Baggett was dressed much as he had been at Leavenworth, a pistol belt and holster his only concession to the dangers of the frontier. And yet, some of the meticulous care seemed lacking; there was, almost, a taint of slovenliness about him.

Certainly, the ease with which he had juggled that heavy demijohn across his elbow — that was not an art he had brought from the eastern seaboard with him. Furthermore, the man Steve had met that first day in the office at Leavenworth would hardly have chosen rough and illiterate teamsters for his drinking companions.

"I didn't expect to see you this far from Leavenworth," Corey told him, his tone without warmth. There was no need now for any pretense, for dissembling the antagonism they had kept buried when in the company of Martin Wilcox.

Baggett ignored the remark. He said bluntly, "You don't need to concern yourself about these wagons. Noonan and I took personal charge of loading them."

"Yes?" Corey looked at the wagon boss. Even across a distance of half-a-dozen feet he could smell the booze the man had poured into himself. A slovenly wagonmaster meant a poorly run train, and Baggett himself sounded thick-tongued and half drunk.

"How about this?" Slipping a boot from stirrup, Corey gave the wheel beside him a hard kick; a hickory spoke rattled in its setting in the hub. "That will lose you a wheel and cost you a wagon, if it's not fixed. And this!" His searching glance had found a loose patch in the canvas sheeting behind Baggett. He kneed his sorrel over and, reaching, seized the strip of canvas; it tore off in his hand and he flung it on the ground.

"These rigs have covered a hell of a lot of ground since they left Leavenworth," Noonan reminded him sourly.

"No excuse! Why aren't you at work now, giving them a thorough overhaul? Don't you know it's October — and we've got a winter campaign staring us in the face?" He turned on Baggett. "Noonan ought to realize, if you don't, what that can mean in this country! It means we're going to lose stock, and we're going to lose wagons. Just how many, will depend on their condition when we start west from here."

"Who are you trying to frighten?" Baggett scoffed at him. "Eight trains and an advance column of troops have already crossed the Green. Others are at South Pass by now. Once the expedition really gets to rolling, we'll be in Salt Lake City inside a week."

"You really think the job is going to be that easy?" Corey took the reins, his face tight with anger. "I think you're going to find out different. Meanwhile you'd better prepare for the worst. Maybe it means nothing to you, because it's Martin Wilcox who stands to face the loss. But I'm warning you and I hope I make it plain: If he loses through your carelessness, Baggett — I'll take every dollar of it out of your hide! Don't think I won't!"

The warning lay like a whiplash between them. Not waiting for an answer, Corey pulled his sorrel back, turning it by a nudge of his heel. He added, with a contemptuous flick of his glance at the litter around him: "And clean up this pig sty of a camp!"

He left them with that, giving the sorrel a kick that sent it away from there, and heading toward the fort. Temper subsided in him slowly. Things had been destined to reach an open break; he was just as glad to have it out, and the differences laid bare.

# 7

He located the commissary office, and together with a mounted detail under a noncom, rode out to bring in the train from Nebraska City. Putting the wagons on the grounds assigned them, outspanning, setting up a temporary camp — all this was time-consuming work, and it was an hour before Corey felt satisfied with the way the job had been done. He left Jorgesen in charge and headed back to the fort, taking Ed Loman with him because Ed still had his precious envelope unmailed. They rode straight to the sutler's, and swung down from their ponies.

Laramie showed a bustling activity, swollen beyond capacity as it was by the nearby encampment and the campaign for which this was the nerve center. Troopers were busy at the stables and the commissary warehouse, where swearing teamsters waited their turns with freight to be unloaded. A stream of soldiers through a certain sentry-guarded doorway indicated the rooms Colonel Albert Sidney Johnston had

低ow what he's talking about, do you
…ink?"

Corey found his tongue, but the words
…eemed leaden in his throat. "Cal Finney's
…ot an easy man to fool! It must be like he
…ays."

Loman's eyes widened. He had heard his
friend defend the Saints, often enough; he
was astonished at the new, chill note that
had crept into his voice. "I never thought
I'd some day hear you admit —"

A sudden rush of pounding hoofs, somewhere north of the fort buildings, and a
scattered popping of guns and ravel of
shouts could be heard. The three turned
involuntarily. In the open doorway a
trooper said, "That sounds to me like
they're headed for the handcart camp."

Steve turned on MacLeod, as the old
Scot's hand clutched at his arm. "What
does he mean?"

"Lad, I all but forgot! It's one of these
Mormon emigrant parties — ye understand? They're mostly foreigners, that
canna even speak good English. The colonel has declared their camp off limits,
given orders they are no to be molested —"

"Orders or not!" exclaimed Corey.
"Sounds to me like somebody's worked up
over the massacre and is out for scalps!"

appropriated as headquarters for his expedition.

A clot of men were gathered at headquarters entrance, swelling as more
troopers came running across the parade.
They could hear the excited pitch of
voices, without making out what was being
said. "What do you suppose is going on?"
Ed Loman grunted, tying his horse. Corey
frowned, and jerked his head toward the
store. Ed followed him in.

The dark room smelled of horses, of
man sweat, of beer and tobacco and the
hundred other needs that frontier soldiers
bought here with their eleven dollars a
month. A couple of troopers were at the
counter, and the clerk on duty, who accepted Loman's bulky envelope. "While
you're at it," Steve asked him, "would you
mind looking to see if you're holding any
mail for Steve Corey?"

The man checked, but there was nothing. Corey told himself he had no reason
to feel disappointed, but still he had been
more than half believing that there would
be some word from Melissa. But then he
reminded himself that if there had been
any message, MacLeod would undoubtedly have it in his personal keeping. He
asked, "Where's your boss?"

"MacLeod? He went over to headquarters, trying to find out more about the massacre."

"What massacre?"

One of the soldiers answered. "There's rumors of some emigrant train the Mormons are supposed to have hit; killed a lot of women and children. . . ."

The second trooper cursed, fervently, as Corey stood stunned under the impact of this. Then his eye met Ed Loman's and he said shortly, "Come on!"

The parade ground buzzed with excitement and mounting anger. Steve was going for his horse, when he caught sight of Andrew MacLeod hurrying up from headquarters, and he turned quickly to meet him. The old Scot looked grimly serious, and when he saw Corey he said, without preliminary greeting, "Ah, lad! Ye've heard the news, then?"

"It's true?" Steve demanded harshly.

"Aye, it seems so. There's a mountain man, just in from the West — his name is Finney —"

"Cal Finney? I know him — he's reliable."

" 'Tis the same," MacLeod agreed, nodding. "He's been to Salt Lake. He reports that the Mormon militia is in the field, pillaging in the vicinity of the Green. burning off the prairie, and he says destroyed a couple of supply trains.

Steve exclaimed, "Wilcox wagons

"I fear so, lad."

Corey heard Ed Loman's exclam thinking of the loss, his own hands t ened to fists. Then Ed was saying, ' what's this about a massacre?"

"The whole Basin knows about th Finney says, but they winna talk. It m have happened about a month ago, som where south of Salt Lake on the Californi trail — a place called Mountain Meadow He saw the evidence, himself, of a Gentile emigrant train wiped out. He learned that these people had made enemies for themselves going through the Territory. The Fancher company, they called it. . . ."

A wave of sick horror engulfed Corey. He thought back to that summer day — to the Owens family, man and wife, and the sunny-haired little girl. He remembered the loud-talking Missourians, and his own dark premonitions of trouble ahead for Fancher and his people. And now, evidently, the premonition had come true.

He turned a blind glance to Ed Loman, hearing the youngster's question dimly repeated. "I said, what about it? Does Finney

He whirled and ran to the hitching post, ducked under it, and grabbed the reins to jerk them loose. As he lifted himself into the saddle, old MacLeod was suddenly beside him, a hand catching at his boot. Steve held the restless horse, leaning to hear what MacLeod was trying to say to him.

"Your girl! She's at the camp, lad!"

"What!"

"She dinna go back to Salt Lake with her brother, after ye left. These people arrived, with a good many sick from the trail. They laid up here to care for them, and she stayed on so she could help."

For a long moment Corey stared at the old man, not fully comprehending what he had been told. Then with a curse he yanked the sorrel's head about and the animal spurted forward as he kicked it into motion.

Dismounted troops, yelling, barely cleared from the path. Sod gouted under the sorrel's hoofs, and Steve had a moment to think that the commanding officer of the fort probably did not much enjoy seeing his carefully tended parade cut to pieces by the irons of a galloping horse. A sentry, halting in midstride, yelled and juggled his rifle; but before he could decide whether he should use it, Corey was past him, and the last buildings dropped behind.

He caught sight of the horsemen, at once — nearly a dozen of them. They were not soldiers. With a sudden hard clarity Corey recognized York Baggett's wagonmen; several were already almost too drunk to stay in saddle. They yipped and yelled, and the late sun winked from brandished whisky bottles and from the guns a few carried openly. Corey scowled, slipping his own revolver; but just then a dip of the ground carried that crowd from sight.

When he reached the edge of the hollow, he could hear from beyond the sudden, terrifying sound of women's screaming, the cursing and yelling of men. The speed of the sorrel took him over the edge without breaking stride, and there directly in front of him lay the Mormon camp.

There were a scatter of tents and cookfires, a few covered wagons, perhaps a couple of dozen of the two-wheeled pullcarts which these Saints had already drawn for a thousand miles over the trail toward their promised Zion. A peaceful scene, moments earlier; but Baggett's wagonmen had burst upon this camp with no warning and were swarming through it.

Frantic women caught up their children from under the very feet of lunging horses. Corey saw a handcart smashed to splinters. A tent collapsed as a horse stumbled into it. He saw a rider deliberately use his boot on the cross bar that held a bubbling cookpot, sending it crashing into the fire. He saw a Mormon who had been chopping wood stand and swing the ax — and receive a ball in the chest. When he fell, the rider drove a second deliberate shot into his lifeless body.

Steve swung his pistol and fired, in a cold rage. The killer lurched sideways, lost balance and went down upon the body of his victim.

A ball whipped waspishly past Corey, but the one who had fired was too drunk for good aiming, or even to hold an uneasy saddle. As Steve tried to draw a bead the terrified horse reared under the man and he slid across its rump, arms pinwheeling. Steve saw with satisfaction a couple of the Mormon women instantly fall on him and disarm him.

The first terror past, the people of the camp were putting up a fight now, even though they had few proper weapons at hand. One, brandishing a smoking billet snatched from a fire, leaped at a raider and took a gun barrel across the side of the head that dropped him senseless; but instantly two more were there to grab the bridle, and drag the rider to the ground. Corey shoved his horse hard against another, and grasping a handful of clothing, hauled a bawling wagonman toward him. He laid his gun barrel against the side of the whiskered head and let the tough drop between their horses.

Ashes of a campfire spurted under shod hoofs as he yanked the sorrel about. A woman's sobbing scream reached him. He saw her; a pretty German lass, dress torn at the shoulder and flaxen hair disarrayed, was struggling in Jud Noonan's powerful grasp. Noonan had the brute strength to lean and lift her bodily to the saddle, and before Corey could reach him he would probably have done so had not a voice called out: "Put her down! Do you hear me? Let go of her, or I'll use this!"

Noonan hesitated, still holding to his struggling victim. And Steve Corey saw the second girl.

She stood with a rifle grasped in small but competent hands, its muzzle slanted up at the wagon boss. Her eyes, defiant in a pale but determined face, held their warning. Now, as Noonan made no move to obey, she pulled the trigger.

The recoil of the heavy weapon almost tore it from her hands. The bullet missed but it jarred Noonan into dropping his prisoner. Fury twisting his mouth to an ugly shape, Noonan yanked his horse toward the girl and snatched the empty rifle from her, pulling her to her knees. In horror Corey saw him swing the weapon, to use it as a club.

He called hoarsely: "Melissa! *Look out —*" At the same time he fired.

The rifle's wooden stock splintered as it was wrenched from Noonan's hand. With a howl of pain, he jerked about — and saw Steve Corey, and the smoking revolver that had him covered.

"Make a move!" Corey spoke through set teeth. "Just give me the chance, Noonan!" But the man knew his peril and would not risk it; he sat there, his thick chest heaving and the black hair streaming into a sweaty face.

And now, down across the low swell above the camp, a line of men in blue were suddenly coming on the double, rifles at high port and mounted officers leading them. And so the trouble was halted, almost as quickly as it had begun.

# 8

As he dismounted, rough hands seized Steve Corey; when he tried to shake loose, one of the troopers at his elbow snarled, "Come along easy, boy, or you'll get a couple inches of army rifle in your kidney!"

Melissa Tyler cried out, and her hands lifted as though to save him. "No, no! Not Steve Corey! He wasn't one of them!"

"Just a moment. . . ."

All their heads lifted, to the saber-stiff, erect figure who had ridden up in time to hear her words. The colonel's insignia on the shoulders of his tunic identified him for Steve, who until this moment had never seen the commander of the Utah Expedition. "You're Steve Corey?" Albert Sidney Johnston gave a signal to his men and Steve was at once set free. "Martin Wilcox wrote me to expect you. Could you report to my headquarters as soon as convenient?"

"Sure." Steve saw a man in his fifties: thin-faced, balding, with fierce swirling sideburns and mustache, and a direct and penetrating eye, an eye that seemed to tally his trail-stained, unshaven appearance, from hat to boots, in a single, inclusive stroke.

The colonel's glance moved on and discovered Jud Noonan, who was sweating with pain as he hugged bullet-numbed fingers to him. "There's one for you," he told his men; the troopers moved to drag Noonan from his saddle and hurry him to join the growing gather of prisoners. Johnston turned to the German girl who stood beside one of the loaded hand-carts, clutching her torn dress about her shoulders. "My sincere apologies," he told her gravely, in his soft Kentuckian's voice. "I was trying to avoid something like this, when I ordered your camp made here out of sight of the fort. You weren't hurt, I trust?"

The German girl, probably unable to understand a word he had spoken, met his piercing glance with a look of terror, and then suddenly turned and fled. Melissa Tyler said quickly, "She's all right — only frightened."

The colonel nodded, in understanding. He looked at Corey again, then touched his hat in salute to the Mormon girl and gave his mount an impatient jerk of the reins. They watched his spare and military figure, unbendingly erect, disappear through the clutter of the raided camp.

And then they looked at each other, and the girl came into Steve Corey's arms.

"Melissa! My darling!"

Her brave defense had crumbled, leaving her shaken and sobbing. "It's all right," he repeated, to soothe her. "The trouble's over." Trembling shook her and then she was still, with her body pressed against him.

"Hold me, Steve! Close."

For that moment oblivious to everything, he lifted his head suddenly and discovered Ed Loman sitting saddle a few yards away, staring at him. The young fellow wore a look of astonishment, but when he found Steve's eyes on him, broke into a grin. He winked broadly, jerked rein and sent his horse loping away among the camp layout.

Melissa Tyler drew back, her hands still upon his shoulders, and lifted lovely, troubled eyes to him. Steve stammered what was uppermost in his mind: "I never dreamt I'd find you here, of all places!"

"I just couldn't leave," she said. "Not when these poor people arrived with their sick, needing me. There are always the sick and the dying, when they've come this far.

The crossing takes an awful toll."

He nodded grimly. "I know."

It was the least expensive way, perhaps, of bringing poor emigrants to Zion, but he had tried in vain to dissuade Brigham Young from attempting the scheme. Last year, misjudging the time it might take a company of pilgrims to cross the plains afoot and pulling, two abreast, at the handles of laden two-wheeled carts, the companies had started too late. They had been caught by the break of winter, and suffered unspeakable privation, and death from hunger and cold.

"And then," Melissa added, looking around her, "after all they've been through — to have this!" Her mouth trembled with pity and with shock.

"It's over now," he repeated, soothingly. "It won't happen again."

"Yes it will," she said, heavily. "I know! This was only a foretaste of what we can expect when —"

Suddenly her eyes seemed to withdraw behind a veil of horror. There was fear in them, Steve Corey realized — fear of himself! Her body tensed, but before she could move to break away, his hands tightened on her shoulders. "Melissa — please! What is it?"

Bitter sobs shook her. "Let me alone! I don't want to see you!"

"No!" be cried. "You're too upset to realize what you're saying! You needn't think I'm going to give you up this easy!" he told her, hoarsely. "Why should it matter to us, if fools and fanatics want to tear the world apart?"

Her stubborn chin lifted; her eyes had gone bright with anger. " 'Fanatics?' " she repeated.

"You know I don't mean you!"

"But you meant something," she insisted, doggedly. "It's in your look — something I never saw there before. It frightens me!"

He knew then that there was no use in trying to deceive her, or himself. He dropped his hands, releasing her. "Maybe so," he admitted, bleakly. "I just learned what happened at Mountain Meadow — about that Fancher train, massacred by white men."

Her eyes widened as she read what was in his own. "You don't? Steve, you *can't* believe —"

"The men who raided this camp believed it," he said. "That's why they came. Being drunk, they didn't bother to think whether there might be any difference between one Mormon and another."

She caught her breath; her glance filled with revulsion. "You're making excuses for them! You're accepting this — this lie about us! You, of all men, Steve, that should know better. Tell me you don't believe it!"

It was she who was pleading, now. But though he tried, he could not give her the assurance she begged of him. He touched his tongue to lips gone suddenly dry. He said, lamely — desperately: "Whatever I think, it doesn't need to have anything to do with us — with you and me!"

But even as he spoke he knew the hollowness of his words, and they died on his tongue. He could only stare numbly as she shook her head, her eyes bright with unshed tears.

"It would always be between us, Steve: you thinking, in your heart, that my people — that we —" Her hand, half raised, drew back without touching him; she placed its knuckles against trembling lips, looking at him and shaking her head a little. Suddenly she turned and hurried blindly away, the full skirts caught up in one hand against her slender figure. And though he tried to speak her name, it choked his throat, and Steve Corey stood and let her go.

An oil lamp burned in a wall bracket above the desk in Colonel Johnston's temporary headquarters, combating the early ending of this brief winter afternoon. Retreat had just been sounded, and echoes of the sunset gun battered away among the hills.

Corey leaned his shoulder against the rough wall near a big map of Utah Territory, and watched York Baggett, reading in his flushed and scowling face the telltale signs of the liquor the man had drunk. When Colonel Johnston spoke, Steve looked at him, seated behind his desk, and saw that Johnston was having trouble keeping a curb on a shortening temper.

"I called you in here, Mr. Baggett," the army man said curtly, hands flat upon the desk in front of him, "not for an argument, but an explanation of the disgraceful thing that happened this afternoon!"

Baggett's eyes, muddied with the fog of drink, flickered slightly. "I can't see that any explanation's needed. The boys were a little high, maybe; then this news hit. You can't blame them for getting excited."

"Can't you? Maybe you'll explain this, Mr. Baggett: You knew they were headed for the Mormon camp, yet you made no effort to stop them?"

Baggett lost some of his composure. "I — that would have been a pretty big order, Colonel!"

"Or even try to get me warning?" Johnston prodded.

Over at the window the portly, clean-shaven man who stood with fleshy hands locked behind him, apparently admiring the sunset, tossed a remark across one shoulder: "Perhaps the gentleman was a little — excited — himself!"

Corey felt a smile quirk the corners of his lips, and even the scout who squatted on moccasined heels in a corner of the room — old Cal Finney adding the stench of smoldering kinnikinnick to the ripe reek of grease-stiffened buckskins — allowed himself a grunt of amusement. Baggett heard the sound, but it was Corey's smile that touched him to anger. His flush deepening, he turned back to the desk belligerently.

"What I want to know," he demanded, "is what you intend doing with my men?"

"I've got the matter under advisement," Johnston told him calmly. "A man was killed at that camp, remember."

"But these are civilians! You have no authority to hold them."

"Authority enough, Mr. Baggett!" the colonel corrected him pointedly.

Alfred Cumming, the man appointed by President Buchanan to the ticklish task of ousting Brigham Young from the governorship of Utah Territory, turned from the window. His fleshy face was beardless and as fair-complexioned as a woman's; he had oddly petulant features, but his eye was shrewd and Corey knew he had a good record as an official in Indian affairs on the Upper Missouri.

"In my view, Colonel," he said quietly, his voice betraying his Southern origin, "this is a case for discipline. Otherwise, as time passes and we come in nearer contact with the Mormons, we're sure to see such incidents; killing, looting — no telling what!"

"So what do you expect?" York Baggett lashed at him. "Who cares what happens to a few Mormons more or less?" He turned on the colonel, the whisky telling now despite his efforts to control it. "You're a soldier. Tell this man a few facts about the spoils of war!"

"War?" Johnston shook his long head, his face stern. "You seem to be suffering under a general misconception. We are not engaged in a punitive expedition. My instructions are to preserve peace in the Territory, and aid Governor Cumming, if necessary, in assuming office. The Mormons have never had a Gentile over them and they may resist; that's entirely up to them. As for whether this will actually come to fighting," he added, a little drily, "I have someone on my staff I consider better qualified to judge than you are!"

He turned to a man who also wore a colonel's insignia on the shoulders of his tunic, and who had been listening silently to this talk from his own desk, in a corner of the slowly darkening office. "Colonel Cooke," Johnston explained, "was in command of the Mormon volunteers who fought for us in the War with Mexico. Personally, I'm inclined to think that he would know more about the Mormon as a fighter than any other Gentile I could name. Or — don't you agree, Mr. Baggett?"

As the contractor scowled, taken somewhat aback, the gray-haired officer acknowledged Johnston's comment with a nod. He said, "I've never commanded better soldiers. The Mormon has a fierce loyalty and a singleness of purpose that can do great things, if they're properly channeled."

Baggett's eyes narrowed. "And, if they

aren't — ?" he challenged.

Johnston told him bluntly, "You weren't called in here to discuss the psychology of a people you know nothing about! To get back to the subject: Those wagons of yours, Mr. Baggett, are not in good shape. I want them taken care of. I want every load examined and, if necessary, re-packed. Is that understood?"

Baggett was jarred erect. He shot a black glance at Steve Corey before he answered. "I'll be damned if —"

"I said, is it understood?" Johnston re-peated, sharply. "I'm not going to waste time offering you suggestions, because I'm quite aware you'd pay no attention to them. So I'm making this an order!"

Corey saw the contractor's face lose a little of its color, saw his full lips tighten. "It could be just a little dangerous, Col-onel! I'd like to remind you —"

"I know: your connections in the War Department!" Johnston shook his head, eyes meeting Baggett's without compro-mise. "But let me remind *you* that this is Fort Laramie — a long distance from Washington, Mr. Baggett. And tomorrow," he added coldly, "you're going to start loading wagons!"

"Impossible! I'm due back in Leavenworth — and you have my wagon boss in jail!"

Cumming spoke up, with a nod in Corey's direction. "What's the matter with this man? Doesn't he work for you?"

"Corey?" A fire leaped in Baggett's eyes; his mouth pulled down hard. "He'll never lay a finger on any of my wagons!"

His ferocity made the governor blink. Colonel Johnston's fierce brow darkened. "Look here!" he snapped, his stare passing between the two freight-company men. "I'll not stand for any personal feuds in my command!"

But Baggett had found here a safer outlet for his temper. He flung a trembling hand at Corey. "The man's a Mormon-lover, Colonel — and I'll tell you, you're a fool if you trust him. You ought to have heard what he was saying earlier today about the way this campaign is being conducted!"

They were all looking at Steve, now, speculatively; anger swelled his chest. "What I said was that we were bound to have losses, trying a winter campaign in such country as this. I said it would be no easy thing to break through Echo Canyon. That's my opinion, and I'll stand by it!"

"My opinion too," Cal Finney put in un-

123

expectedly. Johnston looked from one to the other, his eyes thoughtful.

"Perhaps," he said, "I agree with both of you! But I have my orders, and as a soldier I'll follow them — and I'll demand the full cooperation of every man to help me do it!"

"You got mine," Corey assured him promptly. "Those are *my* orders, from Martin Wilcox."

"And you, Baggett —" Johnston turned on the contractor, and his voice and his face held a finality that did not invite argument. "You'll get your wagon crews sobered up and set them to work. If you need help putting your trains in shape I'll lend you all you want. And if you can't stay and supervise the job yourself, then I'll assign an officer to it. Now, I don't see there can be any objection to that!"

Baggett had torn his angry stare from Steve; his mouth worked and he shrugged heavily. "Suit yourself! It appears we're dealing with a military dictatorship, and not much one man can do about it out here! But you may not have heard the last of this." He sent his muddy glance ranging over all the men in the room. "Not by a long way!" He turned on his heel and strode out.

In the brief moment of silence that followed, Governor Cumming told the colonel, "He can make trouble for you!"

"He can try," grunted Johnston.

He swung to his desk, took up a paper and scanned it briefly, tossed it aside; his mind was obviously not on what he read. He hitched himself onto a corner of the desk, and his glance sought Steve Corey. "Needless to say," he remarked, "I'm not paying too much attention to our friend's extravagant charges — not with that much corn whisky under his belt. What about it, Corey? Will you take over the job on the wagons?"

Steve hesitated. "My second in command," he said, "a chap named Ed Loman, could do that as well as I. Because, if it's all the same to you, I'm a sight more concerned about those advance trains that are already beyond the Green. I heard a rumor that a couple of them had been destroyed."

"You heard right," spoke up Cal Finney. The mountain man had taken the pipe from his bearded lips and was squinting into its blackened bowl. "Two that I seen; no telling how many more. Them Danites are really on the warpath, and an unguarded supply train makes mighty attractive pickings."

"What about the crews?" Steve demanded quickly, "and the stock?"

Finney pursed his lips. "They run the oxen off. Wasn't any killin's that I know of — the Saints took 'em by surprise. They let the drivers collect their personal truck and keep one of the wagons to get 'em to South Pass; then made 'em stand back while they torched the wagon sheets. They left a warnin' they'd come back and kill anybody that tried to put out the fires."

He wagged his head, his long, tangled hair brushing the collar of his dirty buckskin shirt. "One Wilcox & Baggett train they burned had enough food aboard to have lasted this whole army most of a winter, I figure. You should have seen the blaze all them pounds of side bacon made!"

Steve looked at the army man. "That's what I mean, Colonel! I want to get out there! My boss can't afford to lose his equipment, any more than the army can spare what's inside the wagons."

"When would you leave?"

"First thing in the morning."

Johnston nodded agreement. "Very well. Drop by before you go and I'll have a message you can deliver for me to Colonel Smith, at South Pass. He must hold the supply trains he has there until I can reach him with reinforcements. And should you run into Alexander, beyond the Green, I want him told he's to wait for me at the juncture of Ham's Fork and the Black. Finney says the grass should be all right there."

"I understand."

"You know the country well? Good! I've retained Finney to scout for me. Jim Bridger is already working with Colonel Alexander — he's got a grudge to work out against the Saints, it appears, because they took his trading post from him. I know just as well as you do, Corey, that we're going to see bad trouble before we ever reach the Basin; and I have to rely on any expert knowledge I'm able to come by!"

He offered his hand and they shook. "One last question," Steve said, and looked at the bearded trapper who still squatted against the wall — a position that had become more natural to the man than standing, or sitting in a chair. "You brought the news from Mountain Meadow. Is there any chance you might have been mistaken, Cal? Could it have been Indians?"

Very deliberately, with a sour look on his weathered face, Finney shook his head. "No mistake, son. I know Injun sign, and I know white. Some Pai-utes was in on that thing, sure enough — it was them hit the train, and forced it to corral, but they couldn't have done much more by themselves. Them pilgrims wasn't massacreed inside the wagon circle. No sir! They was lured out as sure as you're standin' there — by men whose skin was every bit as white as yours or mine, else they wouldn't have riz to the bait."

"I see."

Finney squinted at him from faded blue eyes, and wagged his head slowly. "I know how you feel, Corey. I used to have some respect for Mormons, myself, but I got none now. You didn't see what I seen; all them poor people shot and stripped and hacked, and then dumped helter-skelter into a pit and buried. Only the coyotes had dug 'em up before I got there, and —" He let an eloquent shrug complete the statement.

Slowly, knowing his face must show all the horror he felt, Corey turned to the officer seated at the desk in the corner of the room. He said, "Colonel Cooke, I'd like to ask your opinion, if I may."

This man who had led Mormon troops into battle, who had bivouacked with them in the field, shared short rations and marched with them under blazing suns and pounding rains on the trail to Mexico, did not answer for a moment. He looked down at his hands where they lay before him on the desk, knotted tight.

"I've been trying to find an answer to that question," he said finally, in a low voice. "Frankly, I don't know — I don't know. I wish to God I did!"

Steve Corey nodded. "Thanks," he said, and turned and walked out into the growing darkness.

The cold breeze of early night felt good, though it could not help the sickness that was deep inside him. He stood a moment letting it blow against him, while he grappled at the tormenting confusion of loyalties and doubts. . . .

"Just a minute!"

Baggett's voice was at his elbow; the man must have been waiting for him. Corey turned hastily, his whole body tensed. Baggett stood half in shadow but the light from a window touched him plainly enough to show the anger in his face. "Did you put the idea in Johnston's head about checking my wagons?"

"I might have," Corey told him sharply. "But it wasn't necessary. The colonel is no fool, and he has eyes of his own." He added, when the other didn't speak, "Now I'll ask you one: Just what did you have to do with those toughs raiding the handcart company?"

"Nothing, of course!"

"It was your whisky," Steve reminded him. "And you were as drunk as the rest. I don't know where a bunch of bullwhackers could have got horses, either, unless you supplied 'em!"

He thought Baggett would hit him. He saw the man's fist raise, tight clenched; but it dropped again to Baggett's side. Fury thickened his voice as he spoke. "I'll tell you for the last time, Corey: stay away from me, and keep your nose out of my affairs!"

"It doesn't matter a damn to me what you do," Steve answered coldly. "Until you hurt my friends, on purpose or otherwise. Meantime I'd like to give you a little advice! You came from the East; I know you look down on me because I don't know anything about your world, and ain't had the advantage of the education you have. But, York, this is a different world you're a part of now; and when those two worlds meet, I've noticed they got a funny way of bringing out the worst in a man. I've seen it happen, more than once — and right now it's happening to you! I can see a difference since that first day in Leavenworth; the men you've picked up with — men like Jud Noonan. The poison liquor —"

"Shut up!" snarled Baggett.

"All right," Corey replied, quietly. "But watch it!"

Baggett, weaving slightly but still with the cloak of dignity clutched to him, returned his look for a moment longer; then with a curse he heeled about and walked away into the darkness.

Out across the parade sounded the rhythmic tramp of boots as the corporal of the guard passed with his detachment. Listening to the barked commands, the grounding of rifle butts, Steve thought suddenly of the people in the handcart camp, of the horror they had endured today, and of the knowledge that these troopers' guns and bayonets might be turned against them as rebels and enemies of the state. He thought of Melissa; the impulse to find her again and try to make her listen to him was almost overpowering. But he shook his head, knowing it would do no good.

Better to think of the job ahead of him, of the trail he would have to be riding tomorrow.

# 9

Three days west of Laramie — beyond South Pass and Green River — the desolate wastes lay night-black around him, with a frigid wind booming beneath the cloud-scud that blocked out all light of the stars.

Steve Corey hunkered tiredly beside his trail-fire, waiting for the flames to take hold as he listened to his horses stirring and cropping at the thin graze, close behind him. He could feel bone-deep inside him the day-long pound of the saddle, and the loneliness of this empty land. Since leaving South Pass he had seen no human being — almost no living thing at all except for the occasional skulking streak of a coyote, the prairie chickens, and the single mule deer he had shot for meat.

The lateness of the season was more apparent with every day that passed. There had been a rime of heavy frost over everything when he woke this morning, and it rattled on his blankets as he shook and rolled them. With midday the clouds had come, bringing the wind. Now he hugged the warmth of his heavy coat and spread his hands to the blaze. A rattle of sage, whipped by gusty wind, filled the night around him.

He thought bleakly that there could be snow not far behind that wind.

From a pile of gathered fuel he took sagebrush and fed it into the flames. The bitter brush took fire, and the wavering circle of light spread wider about his camp site. Corey pushed to his feet thinking to off saddle and to strip the camp things from his packhorse. Next moment he wheeled and a lash of his boot scattered the embers. In the sudden darkness, he dropped to one knee and his belt gun was in his hand; the ghost of his ruined fire lay strewn about him.

At once the cold swooped down on him again.

He knew from the way his animals had stopped their tearing at the grass that they must have heard the same sounds he had — pulse of horses' hoofs, an undetermined number. At once he was on his feet, gun put away, and was jerking reins free of the pickets. He waited with hand on the horn before mounting; he heard no further sound now above the lash of the wind, but he was sure he hadn't been mistaken.

Riders were cruising the night, and they were certain to have seen his fire across this immensity of sagebrush waste. Nor could there be much question who they were. For days he had ridden through the stench of miles of prairie burnt over by marauding Saints until now the odor seemed almost a part of him — engrained in his hair, his clothing, the very texture of his skin. And at South Pass, he had heard more alarming news of supply trains attacked and burnt, and draft stock run off. The Danites seemed to swarm this desolate country.

He lifted into saddle and put his sorrel up the long rise of a hill, where he again studied the darkness but could see nothing. He rode on more or less without aim, only pushing generally westward. His one real concern was not to stumble into the very men he believed were hunting him.

After perhaps one or two miles of such riding, with a pause at every rise to test for danger, he discovered a glow of light over a low ridge somewhere to the south. He pulled rein to stare at it, thinking it must be still another grass fire. It was fire, all right; but it did not spread, the way a grass fire would under this pushing wind. His mouth was hard as he pulled the sorrel sharply over and kicked it into a run.

He crested a hogback finally and the wagons stood just below him, a dreadful and disheartening sight. Two dozen of them burning, making of the corral a fiery circle. The canvases had gone first; now the naked bows formed so many blazing arches above the slower-burning freight stored beneath them. He saw no sign of life; the wagon crew had vanished and the ox teams apparently had been driven off. There was no hope of saving anything.

Steve Corey sat and cursed — slow, grinding, ugly words that burst from between clenched teeth. Then, drawing an angry breath and letting it run out, he took the reins again.

The sorrel didn't like the heat or the furnace roar and tried to shy, but he held it firm. He came down to the burning train and made a circuit, slowly, helpless to do anything about it but look. The wind rushed hard against him, filling the vacuum left as heated air billowed up with the flames and smoke. This wind and the crackle of the fire covered other noises, so that the clang of an iron shoe against rock, very near him, gave him his first warning.

He whipped about. The fire's after-image was black across his vision and he

135

could see nothing clearly for a long moment; and then it was patently too late. He was outlined all too well against a background of fire, while the dozen horsemen who had closed a semicircle on him were, to his eyes, mere vague shapes in the outer darkness.

A voice said: "Don't give any trouble!"

He made out the speaker now, and judged him to be the leader — a spare, intent man with a great brush of beard whacked off straight across his chest and a Hawkens rifle leveled. The man said, "You slipped away from us a little while ago, but we thought it probable you'd be riding this way, if you happened to see the fire."

So he had let himself fall straight into the hands of the Danites. Furious, Corey jerked his head toward the blazing wagons behind him. "Damn you!" he said harshly. "You did this, I guess?"

Before the Danite could answer, a second horseman exclaimed: "Steve Corey!" and came pushing through the ranks, into the fireglow. It was Dan Fox. Steve looked at the broad, honest face of the big man and relaxed a little. "How are you, Dan?"

"You know him?" the leader demanded.

Dan Fox nodded. "Corey and I worked together for the B Y Express, before the

136

trouble started and lost Brigham his contract with the government."

"A Gentile, isn't he?"

Fox admitted it "But not like some others." Dan's look was troubled, however as he studied the captive.

"Perhaps," muttered the bearded leader. "Still, I think we'll take his gun."

It was a tight moment. They had him ringed, and firelight wavered on steady gunbarrels; but Corey was in no mood to give up his own weapon peacefully. The Mormon leader shifted weight in the saddle, a hand reaching. Before it could touch the holstered gun Steve's heel rammed home and the sorrel under him leaped, slamming square into the other's mount.

There was an outbreak of startled shouting, the squeal of the Danite's horse as it was hurled around. And now Steve's lead horse, giving to the sudden tug of the rope, lunged into the grouped riders and scrambled them. Corey found the Colt's handle, hooked it and pulled it up. But just as it seemed he might break out of the net, the barrel of a long gun came clubbing down on the meaty muscle of his upper arm, a solid blow.

Numbed clear to finger tips, Steve's

hand opened and the revolver went spinning in a smear of firegleam. He was thrown half out of his saddle. His left hand found the saddlehorn but the jar of the rope snapping taut between sorrel and packhorse drove him still farther off balance. Fighting to keep his seat, bent offside like that with the dark ground spinning under him, Steve Corey took a second blow across his neck and shoulder. The hat tumbled from his head and, clubbed down, he left the leather in a limp fall.

Cold earth received him. There in sear grass, with frightened horses stamping all around him, he tried confusedly to roll onto his feet. His gun was lost, and his hat. He managed to pull a boot under him and lever himself up, but as he staggered erect his own horse shouldered him from the rear and knocked him forward. He was spun half around and brought up against another mount, clawing with his hands to hold himself from falling. At once an arm snaked down and tightened on his throat.

Lifted onto his toes, choking, Corey struck at that arm futilely but could not break the hold. Some of the Mormons were out of their saddles, now; hands grabbed and held him. Someone said, gutturally, "All right, let go!" His throat was freed of that stranglehold but the others had him fast by each arm. Panting and defiant, he shook hair out of his eyes and glared around him.

"Don't, Steve!" It was Dan's anxious voice, and Dan was on the ground beside him, wavering firelight showing the grave look of his face. "Use your head! There's too many of us; don't make us hurt you."

Corey's stare was without compromise. "You'd burn a man's wagons," he said, harshly. "You'd run off his stock. Why would you draw a line?"

"You don't understand! We've got our orders. We're to make such trouble as we can, and keep our enemies at a distance as long as possible — but we're not to do more than that. Above all were not to kill!"

"I suppose those were the orders at Mountain Meadow?"

That brought a sudden silence. Held by his captors, throat and shoulder muscles aching from the punishment he had taken, Corey looked around into the faces of the Mormons. He saw the leader run a hand shakily down across his bush of a beard.

"So the story is out?" the man exclaimed in a hollow tone. "Then God have mercy on us all!"

"He better!" Steve told him grimly. "Any chance you had of mercy from the federal government was probably lost the day that massacre was allowed to take place!"

Dan Fox stammered a protest, all but incoherent. "You — you can't punish a whole people, for the crime committed by a few! If we ever learn who was guilty, the Church has promised to expel and punish them."

"Sure! The Church would say that —"

There was a curse. Someone smashed him in the face, hard, rocking his head and smearing stars across his vision. As a mere blur of sound he heard Dan's outcry, and the splat of his fist against the jaw of the man who had struck a helpless prisoner. The hands that held Corey fell away suddenly; he braced himself and shook his head to clear it, but before he could move the muzzle of the leader's gun checked him.

"Enough of this!" The bearded man cried. And, as the militia men slowly quieted: "He's only saying what all our enemies probably believe — can't you understand that? Now, somebody fetch up his horse and put him on it."

Corey heard Dan Fox asking, "What do you mean to do with him?"

"Take him along, naturally. He may know things about the Gentiles' plans. Where's that horse?"

Corey, still dazed, had to be helped into the saddle, but a hand on the saddlehorn steadied him. He was aware that his captors had all remounted, and now at a word from the leader they moved away, heading south. Someone had taken over his packhorse. He swung his head, looking at grim faces and at gleaming gunbarrels. The burning wagon train dropped away behind as they crossed a barren ridge; looking back he could see the glow of it for a while longer, but then this faded and they were alone in darkness, and in silence that was broken only by the horse-sounds and the drone of the wind.

Surrounded as he was, Steve had no chance of escape. He had little idea of how long they rode, or how much distance was laid behind them. After a time they came up with other riders, who were pushing along a bunch of cattle. Corey heard the slough of hoofs and click of horns, and the protesting bellows, and knew that this could only be the draft stock from the burnt train. They passed it at some distance; a nervous guard called a challenge: "Who is it?" and was satisfied by the answer they gave him. They rode on, and the slow-moving cattle slipped back and were lost in the deep night.

Knowing that was Wilcox & Baggett stock, Steve Corey's mouth firmed as he mentally added their loss to that of the wagons that had been destroyed. Once he turned his head to ask of the man next him, "What did you do with the wagon crew? Murder them?"

The man he'd asked did not even look at him — Steve could see him faintly, riding with his face straight ahead, a dim blur. It was someone else who retorted angrily, "What do you take us for? There was no killing. They surrendered without a fight, and we let them take one of the wagons and their personal stuff and head back to South Pass. We've got no war with men who are only earning their pay!"

Corey didn't argue. He accepted the explanation for as much comfort as he could draw from it, and did not speak again.

It couldn't have been much short of midnight when they dipped into a shallow canyon and, away to the left, picked up the star-like glow of a campfire. They turned directly toward it, Corey wondering how — riding blind as they did — the Danites had ever been able to locate their camp again in the immensity of the blackness. A wind that had come stronger as the night grew old was whipping the narrow length of the canyon. It blew grit against their faces; paper-dry leaves, torn from a few cottonwoods along the bottom stream, whipped past them as they rode up the throat of the cut with heads lowered and horses restive under them. They crossed the stream, which was only hock-deep and running black and cold, and a narrow trail took them into camp.

The fire had been made in a shelter of boulders, at a place where the canyon wall was undercut to form a level stretch of bank. With the rocks for a windbreak, and the wind lost somewhere in the brush and whipping treeheads, this was an excellent and hidden spot. Corey saw packs and saddles and, further upstream where there was grass, a good many horses on a picket line. Other men were moving about as this bunch rode in; seeing a prisoner, they quickly gathered to ask questions. Corey sat weighted with weariness and listened to the talk, hardly more interested than if it had been some other man they were discussing. He could smell meat cooking, and coffee; and hunger hollowed him out and weakened him.

The discussion quickly ended. At an order, Steve came down from the saddle, stiffly enough. He watched his sorrel and the packhorse led away into the rocks, to be put out to grass. Someone prodded his shoulder, pointed out a place where he was to sit, well within the light of the fire.

"I get anything to eat?" he demanded.

There was no answer, but presently one of the Mormons came with a plate and a cup of coffee. He took it silently and ate alone, intent on filling his starved belly. His glance ranged the camp, weighing the chances of escape and finding them small. Though they left him to himself, they were keeping a close watch on him.

Presently the bearded leader came and squatted beside him. "We'll have to tie you up," he said, roughly apologetic. "Tomorrow we'll see about sending you in under guard."

"You're wasting your time," snapped Corey, irritably. "If I knew anything to tell, you'd have no luck getting it!"

"We'll see." The man got to his feet again. "We'll send you with a guard, to turn you over to the higher headquarters guarding Echo Canyon. That's the end of our responsibility." He signaled, and one of his men stepped in with a rope ready.

★ ★ ★

Corey lay on his side, awkward in the bonds, with a blanket thrown over him for warmth. He would not have thought it possible he actually could sleep, but tiredness had its way with him in spite of the ropes. As soon as he made up his mind that the knots were too well tied for him to loosen, he gave up his surreptitious struggling. He relaxed instead, listening to the talk and the sounds of camp, and the stomp of picketed horses that carried to his ear through the hard, chill ground. The far-away wind and the steady gurgling of the canyon creek wove their monotony of sound, that seemed to swell louder until it engulfed him, presently, in a fitful blackness.

When he woke, some time later, he was frozen and stiff from cut-off circulation. It was still dark; the fire had died to a seething pool of coals now and the camp lay asleep. He stirred, and groaned as he tried to roll off the arm that was cramped beneath him. At once, very close, there was a whispered warning: "Easy! Don't stir them up!"

He lifted his head, craning for a look into the shadows, but could see nothing. Boots scraped against rock, and someone

145

was close at his side. He heard the breathing, felt hands fumbling at the wrists that were tied behind him. A knife-point nicked his flesh. Awkwardly, then, the blade began sawing at the rope and he felt it give, strand by strand.

At a jerk of his wrists the rope parted; agony needled his arms as he drew them out of that numbed position, and rolled over. Enough light was still shed by the coals of the dying fire to show him that his benefactor was Dan Fox.

"Why are you doing this?" he whispered.

"I didn't think you'd have to ask me that!" Suddenly Dan seized his arm. One of the sleeping men had stirred in his blankets, but he settled again, and once more the silence was unbroken except for the constant burble of the stream.

"All right!" Dan told him, his whisper shaky with the pressure of haste. "Here's the knife — you can finish cutting yourself loose." He pressed the blade into Corey's hand, and went on: "Your sorrel's at the end of the picket line, already saddled. I'm afraid you'll have to leave the packhorse — too risky trying to take them both."

Steve had his legs free. He kicked off the ropes, threw the blanket from him. "The guard?"

"There isn't any. We haven't bothered. You can get out easy enough if you're careful. But, hurry!"

Still Corey hesitated. "Aren't you running a risk? What will they do when they find I've gone?"

"Nothing. They can't prove I helped you. Here, take this." Firelight glinted on the butt of a revolver. "It's the one you lost when we captured you. I found it in the grass."

"Thanks."

Steve accepted the gun. He bunched his feet, moving stiffly on cramped legs. But now Dan seemed unwilling to let him go without one further word. "Steve, about this Mountain Meadow business —"

"Let it go! I didn't hold you responsible, Dan — not you personally."

"That isn't enough! Can't you believe — ?"

"There's no time to discuss it," Steve cut him off. "Something I meant to tell you — about Melissa Tyler. She's with a handcart company, heading west from Laramie. They're probably on the road by now. With bad weather so close, maybe you'd want to meet them — see to it she gets in safe."

"Yeah, that could be. Thanks, Steve, for telling me. But now you'd better be moving!"

Corey nodded. And, carrying his gun, he stole into the shadows, leaving behind this friend to whom friendship had proved more than a word.

Getting away from the cup of boulders was a nerve-tingling business, but despite the crack of a cottonwood limb beneath his boot he made it without rousing an alarm. Now the stirring of horses was about him; he groped along the picket line, hunting his own sorrel and finding it just as Dan had told him — under saddle, with even his light bedroll lashed down behind the cantle. He breathed easier; he holstered the gun, gave the sorrel a pat of greeting as he took the reins and freed them.

The temptation was there to turn the other horses loose and so cut the risk of pursuit; but that would have been unfair to Dan after his friend's helping him. Instead, leading the sorrel, he moved some distance on foot and then eased into the saddle. He waited for a long moment like that, straining for a sound, then spoke softly to the horse, and began a slow walk along the narrow canyon trail.

He remembered the crossing; he put the sorrel to it and took it slowly, hoping that the inevitable splashings he made would not carry above the normal racket of the creek. And when on dry ground again, he felt he had at last passed the danger point.

Breathing normally now, he rode ahead. When they had topped out of the canyon, with the dying campfire almost lost in the darkness, he let the sorrel out. A thin gray stain ran bleakly along the horizon's edge, promising dawn. The wind was cold and sharp as a knife; he ducked his head to it, and struck off north and west through thickly swaying sage, laying distance behind him.

# 10

Dan Fox became suddenly aware of singing, and it surprised and halted him a moment, pulling him up in the stirrups to listen. He knew what it meant, but he had not been expecting it quite this soon. Eagerly he dropped back into the saddle and gave his horse a kick, while his eyes searched the wastes directly ahead.

He took a dip into a hollow and came up the rise beyond it. Across a level flat, adobe hills lifted high, the leaden clouds scraping the eroded peaks with their bellies as they ran before the wind. Below, overshadowed by the towering wall of bare hills, the handcart company came on in a long, undulating line that stretched for more than a mile across sear, burnt prairie. As he neared, the marching song grew clearer, the wind snatching it from the lips of these people who sang, in ragged unison, for comfort and encouragement in their endless march to Zion.

Now Dan saw the individual carts — two-wheeled affairs, their boxes piled high

of the line of march. He set Melissa on her feet, and quickly swung down beside her.

The face of this girl he loved was flushed with happiness, but it showed too the signs of fatigue and strain. She touched his sleeve, shaking her head a little, "I just can't believe it!"

"I saw Steve Corey," he explained. "He said you'd be on your way west from Laramie, so I asked and got permission to ride out and meet the company. There's a turn in the weather coming; we'll have to hurry if you're to make it, safe."

Her hand fell away from his sleeve. He guessed at once that mention of Corey's name had upset her; still, he could do things only in his own blunt way. Melissa asked, "But — where did you and Steve — ?"

"Out there." He jerked his head toward the empty lands to the west. "There was a fire — one of the Gentile supply trains. And he — I think he'd have taken on the lot of us if he'd have been able. Maybe I don't much blame him. It's a terrible thing," he admitted, his eyes shadowed, "having to put the torch to all them wagons. But, we've got no choice. It's orders."

"What happened to Steve?" she demanded.

"He was taken prisoner. But —" Dan's

face colored a little guiltily. "He got away again. Don't be worrying about him."

Her manner changed to bitterness. "I'm not! Believe me, Dan, it doesn't matter. He's turned against us. He holds us all to blame for — that awful massacre."

"I know."

Melissa had dropped her head forward, and he could not see her eyes. They stood like that, the horse beside them, the long line of handcarts slowly filing by in a tired column of dust and squeaking wheels and shuffling feet and spiritless voices; yet they might have been completely alone, for all the thought Dan Fox could give to the faces turning to stare at him. He lifted a hand, wanting but not daring to touch the girl's brown hair. And a great tenderness engulfed him.

There were many things he might have said, had he possessed the tongue. Instead, inarticulate with the same dumbness that had made it ever impossible to speak his love for her, he could only stand helpless with a hurt in his eyes that reflected the hurt he knew she must be feeling.

Then, still not meeting his glance, she turned away saying, "I must get back to the wagon. Those poor women need me."

Dan moved his pony about, held the

stirrup as she mounted. She sat awkwardly sidesaddle, hampered by her long skirts; the man swung up behind and his strong arms went around her to take the reins and help hold her place. He clucked to the horse, got it turned, and started it at an easy lope toward the sick wagon, that they could see now far ahead. The girl in his arms, the touch of her hair against his face, started a throbbing of his pulses and turned him clumsy.

Melissa asked, as they rode, "Have you any word from my brother?"

"You'll see him at Echo Canyon, I reckon. He's in camp there." Dan faltered, scowling at words that were hard to speak. "Orson's — changed."

Her hair brushed against his cheek as she turned to look up at him. "What do you mean?"

"I dunno, really. Something about him that — You'll have to find out for yourself! It's all this trouble, I suppose. None of us can hope to come off untouched by it."

"No one but you, Dan!" she cried, in a warm rush of gratitude, and she moved her hand to rest on his that held the rein. "You'll always be the same."

They rode ahead in silence, for Dan Fox could not trust himself to speak.

★ ★ ★

At South Pass, Steve Corey had been told that Colonel Alexander's advance force would be in camp somewhere near Ham's Fork of the Green. A couple of days' riding brought him to the river but it took nearly as long again to locate the place he was looking for, which turned out to be not surprising; when at last he stumbled upon it, he found the site deserted. There was only the litter of torn earth of a large-sized encampment, abandoned nearly a week. Signs showed that the entire command must have broken camp and moved out, north along the barren right bank.

Corey munched some jerky as he considered, hearing the wind that moaned across the waste and tumbled the low clouds. In the sandy grit that swept about him, he thought he felt an occasional sting of an icy pellet. The wind's direction had swung, definitely; it was out of the north, now, and to follow the sign of Alexander's movement he would have to quarter straight into its slamming force. But Corey had a message to deliver and it gave him no alternative. He put the sorrel, protesting, headlong into the steady blast, that wind wearing down both man and horse; with midafternoon, the snow started.

At once his mount was in trouble, as the first white streaks thickened into a blinding, wind-driven screen, and premature dusk dropped upon the wilderness. The sorrel tried its best to turn, but Corey kept it firmly in hand. The storm increased its howling fury; the ground took on a scum of white that soon thickened, making a slippery footing. Unable at last to make out any distance ahead in the gloom, Corey sought shelter in the scant protection of a cutbank, and made camp.

Building a fire for warmth or cooking was out of the question. He broke out his sleeping bag, after staking the sorrel where it might hope to find a bit of grass. His supper, again, was jerky and left-over cold biscuit. Before morning the temperature had plummeted; when sickly dawn broke he was a mound of snow, inside his bag. The storm seemed not to have ceased at all. It took will power to make him crawl out and prepare to ride again.

The drifts were forming deeply — the only sign, now, a wide stretch of trampled openness which the passing of an army had left across the sage-strewn flats. Into the very teeth of the plains winter, Steve Corey pushed doggedly ahead.

It was a stalled and dispirited army he

came upon. Unutterably tired, and feeling that he could never be warm again, Steve rode down the long column, shouting questions, hearing disgruntled answers:

"Where's your commander?"

"How should I know? Up ahead somewhere."

He passed company after company of infantrymen, with slung muskets, huddling about inadequate fires while the knifing winds swept them; trains of Wilcox & Baggett wagons, the teamsters showing frost-blackened faces, the oxen alarming him with their gaunted appearance. At last he located the command post.

Here was a large tent. A fire crackled in front of it, and head-hanging saddle-mounts were clotted nearby. He dismounted stiffly. The order he carried from Colonel Johnston got him past a frozen sentry and into the comparative warmth of the tent, crowded with the officers who had been called to debate a desperate situation.

A harried-looking Colonel Alexander broke off his discussion to accept the paper Steve handed him. In waiting silence he broke the seal, unfolded the paper, and read it quickly through. He rubbed a hand across his chapped lips and sighed bitterly.

"Well, there it is, gentlemen," he announced. "We turn back!"

There was a stir among the others who stood about in the trampled snow and slush that floored the tent. The colonel shrugged at their angry exclamations. "This order was written before Johnston could have received my report. Just the same, it's an order. We're to join his command at Black's Fork junction."

In the general murmur of discontent, one man voiced a grudging admission. "All for the best, maybe. At the rate we were going, I'd begin to doubt we'd ever reach Soda Springs."

Steve stared at the colonel. "If you don't mind my asking, why Soda Springs? It's a hundred miles out of your way!"

"Jim Bridger's suggestion," Alexander explained, with no apparent resentment. "An easier route into the Basin, he thought — swinging north around the mountains, instead of trying to force our way through Echo Canyon."

"Easier for who?" snapped Corey. "Not for the Wilcox & Baggett draft stock, certainly! They're ready to drop now, from exhaustion."

The officer nodded wearily. "I know. We didn't figure on winter breaking so soon —

or on the Mormon militia. They've been hanging to our flanks, every step. They've burnt the grass, leaving no forage for our animals even when they can get down through the trampled snow. I have no cavalry; I can't do a thing to stop the raiders. Night before last they took most of our spare draft stock. Seven hundred head."

Staggered, Corey could not answer for a moment. It was a terrible loss, meaning that fresh teams were not to be had just when they were most desperately needed. Certainly, the miserable, gaunted oxen now in the yokes could not hold out for long.

He shook his head and was suddenly conscious of tiredness, of hunger, of the cold that had settled into every bone and muscle, the snow that crusted his heavy clothing and inch-long scurf of beard. He said, without conviction, "Wilcox & Baggett will do everything it can — that's my purpose in being here. But to me, frankly, this campaign has the look of disaster!"

Tramping outside into the blinding swirl of snow, he heard the commander issue instructions to his staff: "Give orders to break camp! We start south in thirty minutes."

★ ★ ★

Now, at least, the storm was at their backs: there was this much to temper the weary disgust of the men on learning their effort had been to no purpose — that they must retrace every labored step. The army accustoms its soldiers to revoked decisions, and even these weary and half-frozen men could find resources for crude joking as the long, ragged column turned back the way it had come.

But there was no joking among the wagonmen, for in the condition of their teams they faced a desperate situation. Five Wilcox & Baggett trains had been sandwiched into the long column of marching troops. Corey spoke to the teamsters, looked the wagons over for any road repairs that could and ought to be made; but he was most concerned over the oxen. Pitiful, to see them muzzle at the trampled slush trying to get such little grass as remained, after the previous passing of an army and the torching by the Mormon militia.

The supply of grain he carried for his horses was running low; he rationed it sparingly.

Already that first night, when camp was made, the problem of finding dry fuel was

161

an acute one. The column stretched out for miles across the snowy wastes; a few fitful gleams of campfires sheltered by tarpaulins showed against the storm. His own half-cooked rations wolfed, his horse tended to as best he could manage, Steve crawled into his sleeping bag, feeling slightly guilty when he saw how less well equipped many of the others were for this weather.

He had scarcely managed to fight his chilled body into sleep when a rattle of rifle fire, somewhere to the south along the line, brought him out of his bed reaching for a gun. But the shooting had already died, and a teamster, blasphemous from weariness and rage, told him, "Them Danites, damn them! You never know where they'll hit, but it's always at night — just to make sure a man don't get his sleep out even if the cold will let him."

"They kill many?" Steve wanted to know, still studying the darkness.

"None that I actually know of. They're too canny to get in range of our guns. Just want to remind us they're out there, and keep us edgy."

It was some time before Corey slept again, pondering the man's statement and remembering Dan Fox's words: *"Our or-*

*ders are not to kill."* Well, perhaps. At one time he would have believed it. But whenever he tried to think of his former friends, Cal Finney's terrible story of what he had found at Mountain Meadow always came between.

And then the image of Melissa's loveliness rose into his thoughts, and with a shake of his head he forced the vision from him. Too unmanning to let himself think of her now, shouldered with these tremendous responsibilities to his employer, to his government, and to an army fighting its way against the full fury of the winter and the wilderness.

# 11

The military, as in everything else, had notions of their own about managing a forced march. Their thinking, Steve quickly discovered, preferred making the day's distance in a single, uninterrupted hitch, broken only by the hourly ten-minute break to rest the troops. Such a routine was strictly ruinous for wagon teams, and he went to the top with his protest and managed to get it corrected. But the damage had been done long before his arrival.

It left him with the chore of somehow getting five trains of heavily loaded wagons and wholly insufficient draft stock to the rendezvous at the Black where he could hope to find fresh cattle. Somehow he must locate forage for the starving teams in a fire-scorched land buried now under inches of constantly falling snow. He must keep a close eye on every outfit, judging precisely how much more could be demanded from the staggering oxen before they must be replaced, from the dwindling reserves. And for all his vigil and frozen hours in saddle, each bleak dawn found a few more animals dead from exhaustion, from starvation, from the unyielding zero weather.

And always — just out of range of the long rifles or out of sight among the buttes and thin timber growth that spotted these wastes — lurked the Saints.

Even when unseen, they managed to make their presence felt. By contrast with the shabbily clad and weary foot troops, the Danites were well mounted and apparently operated from carefully prepared bases. Contemptuous, taunting, they did not need to kill, but merely hang to the fringe of the exhausted column and drive and harry it on relentlessly. The second night after Corey's arrival, nearly all the army's pack mules had been stampeded and driven off; the next evening he took the precaution of doubling his guard on the big ox herd. Around midnight, unable to sleep, he saddled and rode out himself, an uneasy caution weighting him.

The herders had a fire, where he took a drink of stout, black coffee; then he rode a wide circle looking over the herd. The cattle stood listless with tails to the wet wind; here and there a beast was down in the deep snow — and that one would, he knew, be dead by morning.

He pulled in finally where the slant of a hill deflected the worst of the wind, stripped his heavy mittens, and dug a cigar from a pocket. There was silence around him, with the dark mass of the stock herd shifting on the snowy flats and, farther on, the clutter of the long column with its fires stretching far beyond the limits of vision. Small sounds nearby seemed muffled yet magnified by the unfamiliar stillness.

He was trying to get a wet sulphur stick to light, when he heard the thing that made him throw match and cigar aside, and fumble the cap-and-ball from his belt holster.

In a whisper of horse hoofs breaking the crust that lidded the deep snow, riders were coming cautiously out of the ravine that flanked this slope — how many he could not tell. Quietly he kicked a boot loose from stirrup, stepped down into snow half as high as his knees, the sorrel in front of him. He waited, gun arm resting on the wet saddle, and watched them. They were faintly visible against the fallen snow. Four of them . . . five . . . and more behind.

Knowledge of what they were after drew Steve's mouth down hard, and his finger crimped the trigger.

The spurt of muzzle flame broke up that clot of horsemen, with startling suddenness. He heard muffled outcries, and then someone fired and, as though released by this answering shot, other weapons were probing for him. The sorrel must have been stung by one of the bullets for it suddenly reared, squealing; the clammy reins ran through his fingers and the animal wheeled and slipped to its knees. Exposed though he was, Steve knew he made a poor target whether the Danites were being particular about sparing his life or not . . . whereas, for his part, he could scarcely miss, firing into that closely-bunched group. Legs braced in the slick drifts, he shot and shot again, and brought a horse crashing heavily under its rider.

At the herd, men were yelling and charging toward this spot. A few more balls were loosed in Corey's direction; but with their surprise destroyed, the Mormons seemed to have no interest in a battle. Already someone was bawling, "Pull back! Pull back!" and horses squealed and jammed into each other as their riders tried to turn in too narrow a space.

Remembering the downed Mormon, then, and hoping for a prisoner, Steve went recklessly forward, wading and slipping in the snow. He saw his man, sprawled behind the dead horse, had almost reached him when, from nowhere, a lunging shape loomed suddenly close upon him. He tried to twist aside but slipped. A man leaned from the saddle; he took a gun barrel, hard, across the side of his head.

Steve lost hat and gun and dropped to his knees, dazed. He caught himself on both hands, in snow to his elbows. The cold shock helped to jar the fog from his brain; yet for a long minute he nearly lost consciousness. When his head cleared, the smell of snow was mingled in his nostrils with the sick odor of blood. Just beneath his face, as he propped himself there, was the white pit his gun had made as it dropped from his fingers; he shoved a hand in after it, grabbed the weapon and brought it up.

The man who struck him had gone to his fallen companion and given him a stirrup. His horse, floundering under this double burden, was already into the ravine when Corey swung the pistol and sent a ball after them, without aiming. He missed; the kick of the explosion was too much and it knocked him flat upon his face.

By the time his men reached him and got him on his feet, the raiders were gone. "I'm all right," he mumbled, thrusting their hands away to steady himself. "Somebody catch up my horse."

He knew he had saved the stock herd — for that night, at least. And perhaps the Mormons would be a little warier about another try.

"They won't get 'em!" he heard a voice mumble thickly. "By God, they won't!" And realized with a kind of numbed surprise that the voice was his own.

The long column moved south, so strung out now that the rear guard found itself making night camp at the spot the advance had left in the morning. It was the lagging supply trains that held them to a pitiful, tortured crawl. The storm had played itself out momentarily, but even with the wind's easing the starved oxen could do no more. On the last two days, they had made a bare five miles, all told.

But then came heartening news. The Black had been sighted, and Johnston's detachment camped there, waiting for them.

Weary men, exhausted by their toil and the constant harrying of the Mormon militia, took renewed courage.

Steve Corey spurred his shaggy-coated,

lean-ribbed sorrel toward the camp. He was picking his way through the busy spread of Sibley tents and bustling troops, when a man seated on an ammunition box beside one of the fires caught his eye, and caused him to rein in for a closer look. This was a wild-looking character, bearded and dirty and huddled into mud-caked clothing; but the pad of paper that he held on his knee as he wrote with a pencil stub identified him. Steve exclaimed, "Ed!" and swung down into boot-tromped slush. The young man's head jerked up, and his face lighted with surprise and pleasure.

"Another letter?" said Steve, grinning at the other's appearance — and thinking that he must look at least twice as desperate himself. "You ought to have plenty to tell Bobby, in this one!"

But his grin stiffened on lips chapped and bleeding from exposure, and a bleak hardness came to his face at the report Ed Loman had for him. It could hardly have been worse. The fury of the wilderness and Mormon raiders had been no more sparing of Johnston's column than of his own, or of the draft stock. They had lost heavily, and two trains had had to be abandoned. Listening to Loman's account, Steve could see with sickening clarity that the relief his beleaguered trains had hoped for was no more than an illusion.

He said grimly, "Let's find Colonel Johnston!"

"General Johnston," Loman corrected him. "He got his brevet the day after you left Laramie."

"Well, here's a chance for him to earn that brigadier's star!" Steve Corey grunted. "It's going to take real soldiering, now, to save this campaign from disaster."

Ed Loman stowed the unfinished letter carefully away and went to get his horse off its picket. When he returned, Steve Corey was sitting stiffly in saddle, his look dangerous, his eyes following the figure of a man who was just vanishing from sight among the litter of the camp. Steve exclaimed harshly, "What the devil! That was —"

"Jud Noonan," the younger man finished, with a sour nod. "After you left, York Baggett got him and the rest of that scum out of the guardhouse — convinced Johnston that he needed every trained wagonman he had handy, for this expedition. They're now on good behavior and Baggett's guarantee that they won't cause any more trouble."

"And then, I suppose, Baggett headed

east for Leavenworth?"

"That's the way it went. I will say they've behaved themselves; and I've managed to keep the liquor away from them. Ole Jorgesen and me worked the tails off them putting these wagons in shape. Wouldn't surprise me if the boys didn't wish, before they were finished, they'd stayed in the guardhouse!"

At the command tent they found Brigadier General Johnston and his staff standing about a rickety deal table, that was strewn with spread maps. Colonel Alexander and other officers from the newly arrived column were here, as well, and the civilian scouts — Cal Finney and the half-legendary mountain man, Jim Bridget. Steve saw Governor Cumming, but the governor was keeping out of this military consultation, as befitted a civilian. He looked little the worse for the hardships of crossing the frozen wilderness from Laramie.

Johnston was orienting a map as the freight-company men entered; he straightened, tossing his compass onto the table top, and nodded briefly. "Greetings! Welcome to the council of war!" he said, with heavy irony. "We're trying to decide how much we can salvage out of this campaign.

172

What about those supply trains of yours, Corey?"

Steve shook his head. "Gone the limit — barring replacements, of course, for the teams we've used up. Loman tells me it's the same way with his own outfits."

Johnston lifted a shoulder. "Well, there are no replacements. I'd been counting on a reserve of nine hundred head being held ready for us on Fontenelle Creek. Word has just reached me that they're gone."

"The Mormons?" The general nodded soberly.

Colonel Alexander seemed utterly stunned by the news that had met him, at the end of his desperate march to reach this place. "We've got to keep going, somehow! God knows we can't sit here! If we aren't able to take the wagons, then burn them and pack what supplies we can."

"And how far do you think we'd get?" retorted Johnston. He rapped the table with his knuckles, and fell to pacing. The rest watched him in silence. The general stopped suddenly, his glance lifting to seek out Jim Bridger's bearded face. "What's left of your fort, Jim?"

Bridger, a man of middle years and tough as the mountains that had been his home, shrugged inside his heavy buffalo coat. "Damned if I know, Gin'ral. Ain't been near it since them Mormons run me out. I understand, though, they went and left it empty."

"How close are we?"

The mountain man considered. "Call it thutty, thutty-five miles. But if you're thinkin' of headin' that way, more like than not the Danites have burnt it to the ground."

"A chance we'll have to take," Johnston decided. "We've no other hope of digging in so this army can hold out until better weather.

"Why not face it?" he said sharply, as he caught the disapproving frowns around him. "There can be no thought of attacking, now — against a stubborn enemy, entrenched and on his own ground. We at least have the supplies we carry with us — let's be thankful for that, and make the best we can of an impossible situation." His stare smoldered as it moved around the group. "Or, has someone got a better suggestion?"

He waited, but there was no answer. Satisfied, Johnston nodded. "The Mormons alone we could whip, but not this wilderness. So, before it's too late, we'll commence an immediate withdrawal to Fort Bridger and go into winter quarters."

"If we get even that far!" said Corey, darkly.

"It'll be no easy job. Only thirty-five miles; but, gentlemen, I can promise you it will prove the mettle of this entire command, before we manage it."

A non-com who had just entered saluted as Johnston turned to take his message. "Sir, the captain said to tell you we've found a dead man in the brush. They say it's one of the teamsters. He's been murdered. . . ."

Corey and Loman exchanged a look; they were out of the tent before anyone else. A knot of soldiers and wagonmen was forming. Steve pushed his way through and then halted, staring at the spot where the body lay, snow-covered, on the blanket that had been used to carry him into camp. The corpse was stiff, the blood that had soaked through his clothing around the knife-thrust in his shoulders was frozen, black.

The general asked, "Your man?"

Corey nodded. "Ole Jorgesen," he answered. "One of the best!"

"We figure he must have got too far from camp," the non-com volunteered; "and gave some Danite a chance to jump him."

"I'm not so sure!" Ed Loman's voice was heavy with suspicion. He looked around him. "Anybody seen that redhead?"

Steve Corey caught Loman by the arm. "Who are you talking about?"

"A man that joined the outfit this side of Green River — signed on as a hunter. He carries a knife, and he looked to me as though he could use it."

"Did he have a name?"

"Reno, something like that, he called himself. And I know I haven't even seen him since sometime last evening."

Corey dropped his hand from the younger man's arm, a quick certainty hardening in him. "Jorgesen's been dead at least that long," he said. He turned to the general. "I'll lay my bet that it wasn't any Mormon put that knife in him!"

The officer scowled, shaking his head. "A grudge killing, eh? That's all I need in my command!"

"I'll take care of this one!" Corey turned to the listening men. "I want a call put out for Bill Reno. And, if he is missing, that will be all the proof I need!"

It would have taken time to make a thorough check of a camp that size, but a half hour satisfied Corey that he knew the answer. "Left his victim, took his horse and some grub, and pulled out," he told Ed Loman, bleakly. "With an all-night start there'd be no hope of bringing him back. We'll have to let him go."

He turned then, drawn by the feeling of hostile eyes pinned on him. Not many feet away Jud Noonan stood in the slush beside a cookfire, boots apart, a tin cup of coffee in his hand. He favored Corey with a look of cold amusement, and then lifted the cup to his bearded mouth and drank, watching Corey above the steaming brim.

Corey walked toward him, moved by the hostility that was a physical force between these two. "What do you know about this?" he said, halting directly in front of the big man.

Noonan finished drinking and flicked the last drops from the empty cup. He turned his head and spat a coffee ground. "That one ain't worth answering!"

"No?" Corey studied him. "Someday I'll catch up with that murderer, and before I kill him there'll be some questions I aim to ask him."

"Such as?"

"What was he doing out here, for one thing. For another, why did York Baggett hire him — and why did he pull out of

Leavenworth in such a hurry that night? Yes, a lot of interesting questions."

Jud Noonan's ugly stare considered him, measured him. A cryptic sort of danger lay between them, in that moment. Finally the big man's lips quirked and he murmured, "You're a nosy one, ain't you? Just maybe Reno used his knife on the wrong man!"

Corey drew a shallow breath. "Could be," he answered. "Could be, for a fact!"

Thirty-five miles! On the map, no distance at all; but the clouds which had seemed perhaps about to clear gathered again through the first morning of resumed southward march. At noon the snow began once more, and with it came shifting winds to scour the frozen wastes in a stinging madness. And Steve Corey, feeling the insidious downward plunge of the temperature, knew then that they were doomed.

For a panicky moment he lost his bearings completely and reined blindly through the smother, as he hunted for the train. He all but stumbled headlong into one of the big wagons before he saw it. The teamster was cursing, yelling; Steve could hear the heavy strike of the sodden whip. Hanging to the timbers of his rig with one hand to keep on his feet, a man could scarcely see his lead yokes for the wild swirl of sleet and ice that filled the air between.

What there was to do, Corey did — helping where he could to straighten out tangled teams, or seizing a prod to goad starved oxen to enough expenditure of strength to keep the ponderous, iron-tired wheels turning in the drifts, and the column somehow moving. Time was forgotten, and daylight had become a gloom of semidarkness that early thickened into night. And then the expedition dropped in its tracks — a straggling, stricken column of twenty-five hundred men and four hundred supply wagons.

The draft stock was turned out to graze, but there was nothing for them but the sage and an occasional scrub willow, no shelter for the men. That night it went to three below zero. In the morning Corey knew about what to expect, yet he felt a kind of sickened horror when he looked through the bleak dawn and saw stiff, snow-encrusted shapes of frozen animals dotting the herd ground.

He estimated they had lost nearly half their stock in a single night.

That began a nightmare of a day. The bottom seemed to have fallen out of the thermometer; he thought it must be growing colder hourly. He saw oxen — poor, gaunted skeletons now — heave and lunge under the goading and fall, bringing their yokemates bellowing to their knees. When they fell, they did not get up again.

It was a waste of energy trying to fight them to their feet; he had them taken out of the yokes, hauled clear of the wagons. Still the snow swirled and stung a man's exposed features, and there was no defense against the cold that crept numbingly through aching limbs. Steve rode bundled to the eyes, but he was soaked from the drifts he floundered into whenever he stopped to help with the weakening cattle.

Once as he crossed a spur of high ground the wind sank, unexpectedly; for a matter of minutes the air cleared and gave him a sudden, startling view of the entire column stretching ahead into shifting veils of snow. Steve had to rein in, overwhelmed by the sight: lurching wagons, a snakelike straggle of foot soldiers fighting their way for every yard of ground. He saw men drop, beaten by exhaustion. He saw their companions, unable to help, stumble on to leave them lying, spots of black against the drifts waiting for the ambulance wagons to come along and rescue them before the creeping cold and frostbite could do their work.

The column halted early, through sheer loss of momentum. Troops and teamsters began the heartbreaking scramble for enough dry tinder of any sort to start even the smallest blaze burning. Corey had dismounted, and for the hundredth time was cracking his suffering mount's nostrils free of the long, ropy icicles its breathing had formed, when a man came in search of him along the wagons.

"Been huntin' you for an hour, Corey," he said, his breath a plume before his pinched, blue face. "Three wagons dropped out, back along the line, for lack of teams. Ed Loman wants to know, do we leave 'em?"

"Like hell we leave 'em!" Steve snapped. Nearby a small clot of wagonmen had formed, one holding up a blanket for shelter while another, on his knees under it, tried to worry flame into soaked sagebrush. Corey walked over to this group, shouting orders. "Forget that! We got some stalled rigs to move. You have any oxen that'll still stand up, bring 'em and come with me."

They only stood and eyed him with tired and sullen resentment. The man under the

181

blanket reared to his feet then and Steve saw it was Jud Noonan. "Go to hell, Corey!" said Noonan through bleeding and blackened lips. "I ain't movin' another step! I'm done in."

The words were hardly spoken when Steve drove them back with a single chopping blow. His numb fist felt nothing, but even in the thick mitten it carried steam enough to send the man floundering, on his shoulders in the snow.

"Don't give me trouble, Noonan!" he gritted, merciless. "By rights the lot of you should be in the Laramie guardhouse. You wanted to come along — now you're going to work. So, move!"

Something in his voice or his angry look must have knocked any argument out of them. Slowly, Noonan crawled to his feet. Without another word he turned away and the rest quickly followed his example.

They managed to rescue every abandoned wagon, and all of the trains were intact before Corey would cease driving his sullen men. But it was late by then, and more cattle had died in the yokes and the deep drifts. Weary and dispirited, Corey knew that another day like this could mean the loss of all the trains and supplies — and, in turn, seal the doom of twenty-five hundred troops marooned in the frozen winter, at seven thousand feet.

The expedition had taken cover wherever it could — in scrub willows, or the protection of low bluffs that cut a little the knifing force of the wind. But there was little shelter for the men or for their fitfully burning fires. Across a shallow, frozen stream, a certain amount of grass had been found in the protection of a cutbank, comparatively free of the drifting snow. Corey ordered the cattle driven to this; it might help a little.

Afterward someone brought him word that Johnston was looking for him, and wearily he put his sorrel through the camp to find out what was wanted. A trooper who sat trying to bind filthy rags more securely about feet that were shoeless and bleeding, located the general for him. Johnston stood beside his horse, in a quiet moment between the issuing of orders. His spare and military figure appeared bent beneath the crushing weight of command. But when he saw someone observing him he straightened quickly and nodded a greeting. Corey stepped down. The general said, without preliminaries, "This can't continue."

"Agreed! I've lost better than a hundred

head of cattle since dawn. Of those I have left, not over half will be fit to work by morning. One more day should about finish them."

"And I've got a sick list twice as long as your arm! It's murder to expose troops this way, with the supply trains holding the entire column down to a crawl."

Steve's eyes narrowed in thought. "Let your men lay over in camp tomorrow, then. I'll take what stock is in any shape, and move ahead with half the wagons. Perhaps by working alternate days, I can make the teams last long enough to get us in."

"We could use a layover," the general agreed. "But you'll have no protection. What about the enemy?"

Corey said drily, "You seen any sign of them lately? My guess would be that they've decided to leave us to the elements."

"You're likely right," Johnston agreed, nodding. "We'll try it your way, then. Anything at all, to save strength so we can last it out to Fort Bridger."

# 12

One look at the rig told the story. A skidding, off-balance descent, out of control, had sent the heavy wagon crashing under its load into a snow-scurfed boulder. From the tilt of the bows, Steve knew that one of the big front wheels was smashed.

Men were standing about, helplessly cursing. Tempers had been worn raw by the never-ceasing ordeal, and now he saw real hatred in the stares they turned on him as he rode up. One harshly voiced the thing that the rest were expecting: "I reckon now we got to unload all the freight out of this and try to fix that wheel!"

Corey didn't answer. Debating, he rubbed a mitten across the thick beard that had ice in it where his pluming breath had frozen. He looked at the line of wagons crawling under a metallic sky, past a long ridge crested with sparse, black, naked timber. Men were struggling at the big wheels, trying with their own puny strength to aid the spent and floundering teams. More wagons were behind them.

He took a deep breath, and it was like a knife-stab to the lungs; he judged the temperature to stand at least a dozen degrees below zero. He had driven his crews hard and now, out of compassion for exhausted strength and beaten wills, he told them curtly, "No! We'll leave this one. Cut the teams loose, and let's go on."

Someone swore in astonishment and relief, and they hurried to carry out the order. Corey looked bleakly up at the big, tilted side of the wagonbox, under its double sheeting, and thought of all the supplies within, and the loss an abandoned outfit would mean to Martin Wilcox. But then he shrugged. There were limits to what flesh and blood could do.

At that moment the first shot came, and lead struck canvas above his head like the flat slap of a fist.

He heard a wagonman's startled cry: *"The Danites!"* He saw them, then — fifty horsemen or more who had melted, unnoticed, out of trees atop that long ridge flanking the stretched-out train. He had judged wrongly, after all. The Saints had not left them, but merely bided their time. Now, with the soldiers still encamped and an unguarded supply train helpless below them, they saw a tempting opportunity.

A shout ran back along that skirmish line, and the guns began to bang as the Mormons sent their horses forward. Steve dropped out of the saddle, fast, dragging the tough-jawed horse after him as he rounded the tail of the wrecked wagon. Hastily he knotted the reins about a wheel's spoke, then went bellying under the wagon, shaking off his mitten and dragging up the cap-and-ball pistol from his belt. All along the line, the wagonmen were seeking cover, and now from beneath the stalled wagons a barrage of fire crackled into the sleet.

It was the attackers' turn for surprise. No doubt they had supposed they would outnumber, by two to one, the men of the helpless train — not anticipating that Corey had tripled his crews. The withering fire that rolled along the barricade of wagons must have come as a shocking revelation. On the hill the charge faltered, then broke as the riders pulled rein, shooting back.

Steve Corey ducked as a ball struck the wagon timbers above his head. He thought grimly, *Somebody up there, at least, is shooting to kill!*

He threw off a couple of shots, although it was a long range for his belt gun. Under the forward end of the wagon, a bearded teamster had an army Springfield and was using it methodically — biting off the cartridges with powder-blackened teeth, ramming powder and bullet down the barrel, thumbing back other heavy hammer, absorbing the shocking jolt of the recoil. There were other long guns in the train, but shooting visibility was poor; the lashing, hissing downpour of sleet beat smoke and stink of powder downward about the stalled wagon wheels. Steve saw a saddle or two emptied. The fallen men seemed only to be wounded, though, or thrown by nervous horses on the slick footing, for in each case he saw them scramble up and head for the cover of black timber.

A mount was hit and went down, the rider managing to throw clear. Through the storm Corey watched him, an indistinct figure, as he pulled himself slowly to his feet. He seemed to have done something to one of his legs. He began a lurching, limping hobble toward the protection of the trees. Steve's neighbor muttered something and swung his rifle barrel, tried a shot at him; it must have come close, for the hobbling figure redoubled its efforts.

But the distance to the trees was too great. The man changed his course and dragged his hurt limb to a down log instead, flung himself behind it.

There was only one possible end to such a battle. The wagon-train defenders could not be knocked out of their entrenched position, and the attackers must have known, from the first break of shooting, that they had tried for game too hard to bag this time. For some minutes the ragged, ineffectual shooting ran on; then as their guns emptied and the spirit lagged in them, the Saints were pulling back. The crackle of fire thinning out, Corey lowered his smoking pistol and watched the line of horsemen melt into the timber. They were gone as quickly as they came.

The man beside him said, "We drove the dirty skunks off for fair, that time. Only wish I could have got a decent shot at one of them!"

"Find out if anyone was hurt," Steve ordered, and reached for his buckskin pouch of powder and shot and caps. Icicles of frozen breath rattled in the other's beard as he nodded, and crawled out from under the wagon to hurry on his errand.

While he re-charged the chambers of his pistol, Steve found his attention returning to that windfall up on the flank of the ridge.

He had seen no movement. The man might have reached the trees somehow without his notice, but if so he could be caught, up there — forgotten by his companions, afoot and hampered by an injured leg. In this weather there was no question what such a predicament would mean; and though it was an enemy, common decency wouldn't allow him to leave any man to his death.

Pistol re-loaded and ready, he crawled back to get his horse, mounted, and struck directly toward the ridge. He approached cautiously, eying the curtain of timber. Nothing moved behind the down log; he was not too surprised when he reached it and found that the hurt man was gone. His track showed plainly, extending toward the trees; and there was the telltale mark gouged by the dragging foot.

Steve went on, tensed and waiting for a bullet or a glimpse of the man. He reached the trees and halted. He heard only silence and the hiss of sleet that slashed at bare branches and undergrowth. The sign pointed straight toward the heart of the thicket. Looking that way he could see no movement, though once he thought he heard a thrashing of splintered branches such as a wounded animal might make.

He called out, "Hey!" and waited a moment but got no answer. "You're hurt," he yelled, trying again. "You can't last long out here, without help. Toss your gun over to me, and I'll see what I can do."

There was no sound from the deep brush, yet he had the strongest feeling that the man was crouched there, breathing shallowly, waiting for a shot at the one who would help him. Steve felt a strong impulse to turn back and leave him to his fate; instead, he stepped down from the saddle, tethered his horse, and moved cautiously forward with the pistol leveled and ready.

The voice, when it came, was startlingly near, though its direction was lost in the gloom and the hiss of sleet: "All right, Corey! I'm looking at you. Don't walk any closer!"

He dropped flat, into the protection of screening brush; the breath caught in his throat as he crouched there. Astonishment gripped him, for he had recognized that voice beyond all likelihood. "Orson!" he called, uncertain where to pitch his words. "Orson Tyler! Is that you, boy?"

Getting no answer, he straightened slowly to his feet, his glance searching. "Where are you?" He took a step, and then another.

A gun roared. Lead clipped from a tree trunk within a foot of his head, and Steve's quick plunge for cover was greeted by mocking laughter that mingled with the dying gun-echoes muffled by the storm.

"I could have put that one right through your hatband!"

Flattened against the tree trunk, Steve yelled, "What the hell's got into you? You and I have no quarrel!"

"No?" came the voice of Orson Tyler. "Want to try sticking your head out again where I can see it?"

Not trying to understand what could have caused this change in one he had called his friend, he concentrated on locating Tyler's position. Somewhere to the south of him, he thought; Corey made a whirling leap and went at a fast, bent-over run to another tree. He had drawn no second bullet.

He paused a moment, listening for sound of the lamed man. He heard nothing. It was an eerie business, this stalking and being stalked through the cold and icy patch of woods. He picked other cover and went toward it in a sudden dash. While he was still in the open the gun roared again and ice gouted in front of his boots. The laughter followed him as he brought up, panting, against the rough, wet bark. "Come ahead — Gentile!"

Steve's patience snapped. "Damn it, Orson!" he shouted. "You got an advantage! You know I wouldn't be able to kill you, even if I had the chance!"

"Why not?" came the retort, somewhere plaguingly close. "On account of Melissa? You still think you stand a show with her?" This time the laugh was harsh and jeering. "You can forget it, then. Because she's married!"

A sensation, something like a cold fist slowly clenching, squeezed deep within Corey. He could not have spoken, just then; after a moment's impatient waiting young Tyler challenged him, in a louder tone: "Didn't you hear what I said? Melissa was sealed to Dan Fox, two weeks ago — right after she got back from Laramie."

"I — I don't believe it!"

"Yes you do! You know I wouldn't let my own sister marry any Gentile!"

Steve Corey dragged in a deep breath, recovering from the first numbing impact of the news. He said, in a leaden voice, "I just don't understand you, Orson. You and I were friends. . . ." He waited, expecting an answer but getting only silence. After a moment he lifted his head, peering ahead through the mist of his own breathing. "Orson?" he repeated, louder.

"Throw away the gun," said the voice calmly — so near that his whole body jerked with stunned surprise. He turned his head. Orson Tyler stood with a shoulder against a tree, weight eased off his hurt leg. The weapon in his hand had Corey covered. However he had managed to sneak around him, Orson had taken him so thoroughly by surprise that there was nothing to do but toss the pistol away, into the snow. That done, Steve could only stare at this young man whose good looks, beard-clouded now, resembled so much those of his sister, though subtly lacking Melissa's strength. There was a change in him, something in his eyes and the bitter lines of his mouth that Steve had never seen there before, and that wasn't altogether the torment of his injured ankle.

"Friends?" Orson repeated. "Us?" He shifted his weight slightly and pain fluttered across his face. "Maybe we were. Maybe that's the reason I'm hesitating about putting this bullet in you, now!"

Steve realized with a certain satisfaction that he felt no fear, even with the black muzzle of the gun pointed at his head. He said harshly, "Dan told me there'd been an

194

order issued: 'No killing.' "

The other ignored him. "Right now," he said, "you're to stay where you are, understand? I think I tore a ligament when that horse went down and it's killing me. You left a horse tied back there. I'm taking it."

Corey looked into those other eyes, darkened by danger and fanaticism, and scarcely the eyes that he had remembered. Then he shrugged. "I don't see how I can stop you."

"Neither do I, for a fact!"

Cautiously, then, Tyler began to withdraw — moving backward, favoring his hurt leg. The sleet fell suddenly harder and he became a wraith that quickly merged with the gloom of the timber. Like a man in a trance, Steve picked up his gun and returned it to its holster. He supposed he could have gone after the hurt man and perhaps stopped him, but probably not without a killing. For the sake of other days — and Melissa — he did not.

Melissa — married! Somehow he felt no resentment, either toward her or to Dan Fox. There was only the numbness of a heavy blow his spirit had not yet fully absorbed. The torment, he supposed, would come later.

He turned, and started walking out of

the trees, toward the slope and the wagons below.

Those last terrible miles, with their starved cattle reduced to the bare number sufficient to draw a single train, they somehow managed to struggle forward as much as three miles a day, with the most desperate and superhuman effort. Looking back, Steve tried to tally the days of suffering, but they melted insensibly together in an endless time of heartbreaking toil and near-despair.

Ed Loman, who had never failed even through the worst of it to add a few lines every evening to the log he kept for his sweetheart in Nebraska City, enabled Steve to straighten out the passing of time. Two weeks, he said, since Johnston gave the orders and started them south toward the hoped-for haven at Fort Bridger. Two weeks, to manage a distance of a mere thirty-five miles!

Steve's determination to get through without abandoning more of the precious outfits had finally gone the way of all impossible hopes. Like the teams, the big freight rigs could not meet the demands that had been forced upon them. One by one, as timbers gave way at last, or oxen fell lifeless under the yokes, wagons had to be dropped from the struggling line. Truly, Steve knew there would be a fearful accounting when they reached the fort. *If* they reached it, he sometimes found himself thinking from the deepest pits of his exhaustion and near despair.

Cal Finney, bundled to the eyes against the cold, rode up on his tough little mountain horse that had eagle plumes woven into mane and tail, Indian fashion, and told him drily, "Well, she's just ahead."

Corey did not even understand him for a moment. "Bridger?" he exclaimed.

"Yep — and is Old Gabe fit to scalp! Ain't nothin' left of it," he explained to Steve's questioning look. "Burnt to the ground, when the Mormons pulled out!"

It was the crowning blow. Steve spurred ahead to see for himself, and so came in sight at last of the place it had cost them so much to reach. Jim Bridger had picked the spot for his emigrant trading post very well indeed, in this broad and watered valley where the great trail made its forking to Oregon, north and west, or on to California through the Salt Lake Basin. But now, there was nothing. The Saints, in making their withdrawal, had done a thorough job. All the log structures Old Gabe had built were in ashes. The Mormons had, however, built a fifteen-foot wall of stone and mortar about the fort, as well as a second, smaller enclosure; and these still stood. Steve was looking them over, with an eye to their possible utilization, when the first wagons took shape through the dusk of a cold day's end.

It was not yet the finish of the job. Days later the army's rear guard and the last of the Wilcox & Baggett wagons were still straggling in, and going into temporary camp. Under Corey's supervision the freight was being unloaded as fast as it arrived, and stored against the walls of the larger enclosure. But before the first wagon had been more than half emptied, Johnston's supply officer was already at Steve's elbow, impatient to be at the contents of the big wooden crates.

"You possibly don't understand," the officer said, "how desperately in need of everything these men are. Boots, blankets, overcoats —"

"I'm sorry, but according to the manifest this first rig has nothing in it but camp kettles."

The other man frowned. "That won't do me much good!" He pointed. "How about the one just coming up?"

"An ammunition wagon," Steve told him. "A special zinc-bottomed outfit."

The officer shrugged and turned away. Over his shoulder he said, "Soon as you get to something I can use, let me know, will you?"

"Certainly." But already Steve Corey was beginning to have his misgivings, which were confirmed when he had looked over more of the train books and manifests. Plainly there had been bungling here that threatened trouble.

His report of the first day's unloading brought the officer back again, and this time he had General Johnston with him. There was danger in the general's sharp eyes, as he held out the papers Corey had dispatched to his tent. "I don't understand this, Corey!"

"I'm afraid it's simple enough. The quartermaster at Fort Leavenworth seems to have loaded these supplies at random, filling each wagon with whatever he had on hand at the moment. Nothing wrong with that, except he didn't make allowance for some of the wagons not getting through!

"If I'd been there," he explained, "or Martin Wilcox, we could have prevented this and seen to it the goods were better distributed. But York Baggett was in charge, and York doesn't know anything at all about the freighting business."

Johnston was nearly white with anger. "It should be enough for a court martial!" He referred to the list in his hand. "Fifteen hundred pairs of epaulets, and some of my men actually barefooted! God knows what we're going to find in the other trains, when they get here!"

"We can only trust to luck. Approximately a third of the wagons we started with were lost, including that one Cal Finney reported burnt with some three hundred thousand pounds of food we're going to wish we had. That gives us two chances in three that the rest will yield something we need worse than we do epaulets and camp kettles!"

One by one the lagging trains limped in, the few oxen that hauled them now hardly able to stagger under the yokes and drag them the last miles to the flat where the fort stood. The snows had ended, and the sky was startlingly blue above an unbroken white dazzle; but it was cold, cold! The small yellow sun gave no heat at all.

The work progressed. As the wagons were unloaded Steve ordered them disassembled and their timbers and canvas used to build shelters and roofs to protect the supplies, stacked within the larger of the two walled enclosures. On the other, lunettes had been built and mounted with cannon, while a garrison dug in to man them and protect the vital store of provisions. What was left of the cattle were gathered and driven to winter on Henry's Fork, under guard of another force commanded by Colonel Cooke himself; these would be slaughtered for meat, as needed.

A camp, meanwhile, had been located for the bulk of the expedition some three miles from the Bridger ruins, on Black Fork where there were steep, sheltering bluffs, water in plenty, even cottonwood for fuel. The Mormons had tried to burn the trees but failed because of the greenness and dampness of the bark. Here the cone-shaped Sibley tents were pitched, and the army dug in. In honor of the aged chief of staff in Washington, Johnston had given these improvised winter quarters the name of Camp Scott.

When the last wagon had been emptied, and Steve rode over to hand his final report to the general, an emergency meeting of Johnston's staff was called at the command tent. An atmosphere of gravity lay on the officers who gathered to receive the grim news.

"Here's the situation," Johnson told them brusquely, hands white-knuckled as they held the sheaf of papers. "For an army of twenty-five hundred we have at our disposal not quite half enough overcoats to go around. We have also been supplied with exactly eight hundred pairs of boots and seven hundred blankets. And as for those blankets — Orderly, bring me one of them."

A trooper came and placed a folded blanket on the table before him. As the group of men watched, Johnston shook out and spread it for them. It bore the U.S. Army stamp, but it was the poorest kind of shoddy. The general took the material between his hands, and under the probing of his fingers the cloth began to separate as the threads loosened.

"Let me see that!" exclaimed Corey, hoarsely. Taking it, his hands were stiff and his gaunt face terrible.

An officer demanded, "Is this the kind of goods Wilcox & Baggett use to fill their contracts? There ought to be a complete investigation."

"There will be," Johnston assured him, bleakly. "I can promise that!"

"What about our food supplies?" someone wanted to know.

"There we come off a little better, fortunately! But only a very little better. I estimate perhaps a hundred and fifty days' rations of flour, about the same of tea and coffee; plenty of beans, dried vegetables, and sugar to see us through to spring. On the other hand, there isn't a pound of salt in camp."

In an appalled silence, Steve Corey spoke his decision. "I'm going back, General."

"To Leavenworth?"

"If there's any possible way to get more supplies through, I'll do it; if not, I'll at least see that they're ready to move at the earliest possible moment after the spring dry-up."

"You actually think you can get through?" the general demanded.

He shrugged. "I'd as soon freeze on the trails, as sitting around Camp Scott. I'd like to take this with me," he added, grimly, and indicated the blanket. "I want Martin Wilcox to see it. I give you my word, General, he knows nothing at all about this."

"You blame his partner, then?" Johnston's look remained bleakly noncommittal. "As far as I'm concerned, that's something for an investigation to decide. Good luck to you, Corey. You'll be able to leave soon, I hope!"

Steve nodded. "I've already given Ed Loman his instructions to carry on for me." He added, "I've got an important document in my pocket to be delivered for him at Nebraska City. Any message that you want me to take?"

The general looked at him, and at the blanket. But whatever he was thinking he shook his head. "No messages. Just get your own self through!"

# 13

A tall Christmas tree brushed the living-room ceiling of Martin Wilcox's home in Nebraska City with its tinsel star, spread a glow of candlelight through ice-rimmed windows to welcome Steve Corey. He reined up and sat for a moment hunched against the night wind that blew along the Missouri River bluffs — too unutterably weary to dismount, and not eager for the scene that probably awaited him inside. Then he swung down, tied his horse to the ring of an iron post, and walked with boots squealing across the packed snow and up the porch steps.

Through narrow windows that flanked the door he saw the stairs and balustrade, shining with new varnish. Holly boughs hung above the curtained archway that led to the living room off the entrance hall. Waiting for an answer he thought of Barbara Wilcox, whose young hands had busied themselves with this decoration.

Then the curtains of the archway stirred and Martin Wilcox appeared, saying something across his shoulder and laughing good-naturedly over the answer he heard from the living room. The laugh was still on his face as he swung open the door; it faded to astonishment.

"Steve!"

"Hello, Martin."

He had had a shave since hitting town, but his clothes were unchanged and the stains of travel lay both upon them and on himself. Martin Wilcox said gruffly, "Steve! I thought you were a thousand miles from here!"

"I was, not too long ago," Corey answered drily. "Right now I'm on my way to Leavenworth."

"And half dead, I'll warrant! Come in man — come in!"

Steve stepped across the threshold, unbuttoning his heavy coat. Martin Wilcox had closed the door, and he helped him shuck out of it, took the hat Steve handed him, and hung both on a peg rack by the living room archway. There was a quick tapping of heels along the upstairs hall and a girl's bright voice called down, "Who was it, Daddy?"

"It's Steve, Baby," bluff Martin Wilcox answered his daughter. "Back from Utah — and in the middle of winter! I'll never know how he made it!"

There was an exclamation, and next moment Bobby Wilcox was at the head of the steps, bending to look down at them. Her red lips were parted, her blue eyes wide. She held up her full skirts in one hand and the other bare white arm was extended to the balustrade for balance. Poised there, she seemed half child and half provocative woman.

Steve grinned at her. "Hello, Bobby." Seeing her searching glance travel past him he added, "No, I'm all alone. But I brought you something."

She crinkled her nose at him. "I'll be down in just a minute," she said, and was gone in a swift swirl of skirts.

Martin had his arm, steering him toward the archway. The curtains dropped behind them; by the soft glow of Christmas-tree candles and a burning log that roared in the deep stone fireplace, he saw the man who stood with elbow against the mantel, a half-finished cup of fruit punch in his hand. York Baggett returned the look, and it was as unreadable as Steve knew his own must be.

Martin Wilcox missed anything that passed between the two men. He went directly to a sideboard where the punch bowl held its jewel of rich red, and poured a drink for his new guest. "Some Christmas punch, Steve? That will warm you up."

"Thanks."

Still not speaking to Baggett, Corey let himself onto the horsehair sofa that faced the fireplace. The punch was good, and spiced to suit even Baggett's taste. The warmth of the blazing fire, and the soft glow of the tall tree in the corner of the room had a lulling pleasantness. He sank into the comfort of the sofa and for a moment sat with eyes closed, every tensed muscle and nerve relaxing.

Wilcox had seated himself in a deep leather-slung chair. He said now, in a different tone, "Something's wrong, isn't it?"

Steve nodded, turning to him. "Plenty. Johnston's stranded at Fort Bridger with about half the supplies he needs to last until spring thaw. I managed to buck my way through, but winter has closed the trails as far as wagons are concerned."

"But — all those supplies were sent ahead! Were our losses so heavy, Steve?" The older man's face had gone ashen.

"Nearly a third."

"Well!" York Baggett's exclamation held a note of triumph and amused scorn. "This is interesting, I must say! Where's the genius who had the responsibility of getting those trains through?"

"Just a minute, York!" Martin Wilcox exclaimed.

Staring up at the sardonic look of the man by the fireplace, Steve willed himself to his feet, across the rag throw rug between them, and into a solid swing of his fist against the middle of that sneering, full-lipped mouth. He almost felt the shock of the blow in his knuckles and shoulder; but the moment passed and he was still there on the sofa, the punch glass in his hand. He said icily:

"I intend to make a full report, Baggett. The cattle the Mormons ran off we may yet recover. A bill of particulars on the other stock and equipment can be drawn and presented to the government." Steve rose and walked to the sideboard with his empty glass, set it down. Turning then, his back against the wood, he looked at Wilcox. "How's your credit these days?"

His old friend lifted a shoulder. "You ought to know. Stretched about to the limit."

"We'll have to stretch it further. Between now and spring we're going to need new wagons, teams — everything. And have them on the road to General Johnston the minute the thaws break."

He saw the heaviness come into the freighter's aging face. Martin Wilcox rubbed a hand across his mouth and his eyes were veiled with thought. He nodded. "All right. We can do it, I guess." His eyes lifted to Steve. "Though you probably realize it will mean a terrific piece of work for you."

"For you too, Martin." Steve braced himself, against the storm he knew he was about to raise. "One of us is going to have to take over the Leavenworth office."

From the corner of his eye he saw York Baggett's head lift with a jerk, from the glass he had half-raised to his lips. Baggett said, "What are you — ?"

Briefly, Corey told of the carelessness that had been discovered on unloading the trains at Bridger. "A man who knew what he was doing," he finished, gruffly, "would have seen to it those supplies were distributed in the wagons in some kind of proportion. Then the loss of one or two — or even a third of them — needn't have meant disaster."

York Baggett's face was a mask of anger. He slapped his punch glass upon the mantelpiece. "Damn you, Corey! I've had enough of your —"

Then he was striding toward Steve, his

clenched fist lifted. Steve waited, not ready to yield ground even if it meant a fight here in Wilcox's house. He heard a frightened gasp that told him Bobby Wilcox must have entered the room, unnoticed.

Stepping quickly, Martin Wilcox edged into the way and caught Baggett's raised arm. "Stop it, York! Steve's right about this. I count it my fault, for not having given you warning about problems you might face at Leavenworth."

The burning log cracked and popped. York Baggett's breathing sounded loud as he glared at Steve past the intervening shoulder of his partner. Over by the archway, Barbara was standing with a hand lifted to her throat; her shoulders and arms were waxen in the soft glow of the candles.

"I'm not quite finished," Corey said harshly. "There's something in my saddlebag that I want to show you, Martin, something that will help you to understand just what kind of a man you're hooked up to!"

He turned on his heel and walked out of the room, outside to his waiting horse. He returned carrying a blanket; he saw the look that crossed Baggett's face. Without a word he handed the thing to Wilcox, and waited while the old man looked at the sleazy material, frowning. Wilcox lifted his head, ran a perturbed look at his partner and then at Corey. "I don't understand this, York!"

"Neither does General Johnston," Steve told him. "He's going to call for a full investigation to explain it."

They were all looking at Baggett, then. And Baggett's jaw clenched hard. "I know nothing at all about this!"

"You're lying!" snapped Corey. "You know all about it — and you've dragged Martin Wilcox into the mess with you! I warned you, Baggett —"

"Cool down." York's manner altered subtly. A sneer touched his mouth, "There's no danger! Do I look like a fool? I've kept the tracks covered. I contract for supplies; I'm not to blame if the manufacturers switch me shoddy goods! There's not a way in the world they can pin anything on me!"

It was a bland and open admission of guilt. Hearing it, an icy calm settled over Steve. "And the men out there in the wilderness? They count for nothing?"

Baggett shrugged. He was red of face and talking loud, now, talking carelessly. The Christmas punch could not have made him as drunk as Steve suddenly knew he was; he must have carried some of his whisky here with him, under his belt.

"You don't expect me to lose sleep over some eleven-a-month private? Any man fool enough to join the army can take his chances. I don't pull my sights off the main target, for anybody or anything!"

"No," Steve retorted. "I don't imagine you'd let anything interfere with the profits you're taking out of this war!"

"This penny-ante expedition of Johnston's?" Scorn edged Baggett's words. He shook his head, and his mouth was an ugly shape. "Don't make me laugh, Corey! This is just where I make my stake and consolidate my position with the military. The *next* war will be the cleanup!"

In a shocked silence, Martin Wilcox repeated huskily, "The — *next* war?"

"Sure — when the Union breaks in two. Give it three years. If the abolitionists can get a man in the White House next election, the South will be forced out — and that'll be the biggest opportunity a man ever had thrown in his lap!"

He looked around him. Perhaps even through the whisky he sensed that he had said too much. But he had gone too far to turn back and now he laughed, mocking their horror. "I see I've shocked you. Or maybe you think my prediction's wrong? Well, put it down, and remember it, when the fools are spilling out their blood and I'm piling up my millions in government contracts!"

Steve drew a slow breath. He said tightly, "I hope you'll excuse me, Martin, I won't stay in the same room with this man!"

"Don't bother!" said Baggett, jeeringly. "I was just going."

He walked steadily enough to the archway. He bowed to Barbara, and seemed amused when she drew back from him; he turned then, and spoke to his scowling partner.

"We'll get together in the morning, Martin," he said, pleasantly, "and discuss this new batch of supplies we need."

He nodded and was gone; they heard the outer door slam behind him. Martin Wilcox's face was working spasmodically. He opened his mouth, trying to speak. Then, without a word, he jerked about and went out of the room. The curtain of the archway fell in place behind him, and a moment later his heavy step was heard slowly mounting the stairs.

Barbara said, in a choked voice, "Poor Daddy! He must feel terrible!"

Corey nodded. "It's been a sad awakening."

She came to him, in a quick whisper of rustling skirts. Her bright head tipped back to meet his eyes. "Can't he break free somehow?"

"I don't know. He's in deep — deeper than he realizes." But then, seeing her anguish over a thing she could not help and was too young to understand, Corey relented; he let a smile soften the hard line of his mouth, and put a comforting hand upon her arm. "We'll think of something. I won't let Baggett drag him under!"

"I know you won't, Steve!" It was her nature to accept uncritically the word of anyone she trusted, and Steve Corey was one of her very oldest friends. Under his assurance, Bobby Wilcox seemed to forget her misgivings — to throw them aside with a gesture as light as the swish of her apple-green skirts, as she turned from him to the sideboard where punch bowl and glasses stood.

"Let me," said Steve, quickly, and poured a cupful for her. She curtsied as she took it, laughing. Had she dressed up for him, or had it been for her father's company, for York Baggett? It really didn't matter. His smile warmed as he admired her fresh beauty, the lithe young body which, in the line of waist and bosom, was disturbingly no longer a child's.

"Oh, for goodness' sake!" she exclaimed, turning to him and wrinkling her nose. "What have you men done to this?"

He laughed and took the glass from her and set it down. "Don't be too hard on us. Remember it's Christmas; and we think it tastes better this way."

"Well, I don't!" But she laughed with him — as a child laughs, wholeheartedly. And she gave Steve both her hands, without question, and let him draw her toward the big sofa facing the fire.

"Come on!" he said. "Sit down here and tell me about yourself. I need cheering up."

"But there isn't a thing to tell!" she protested. And at once launched upon an enraptured account of all the exciting things that had been done and witnessed, in the months since she and Martin Wilcox had come to Nebraska City.

Steve leaned back and let her talk, enjoying himself thoroughly for the first time in unnumbered terrible weeks. There would be time enough for him to tell her a little — a very little — of what he had himself gone through, and all the things she would be wanting to know about young Loman, whose letter he could feel bulging a pocket of his coat. Right now the music of her voice was comfort enough to put, for a time, all the weight of past troubles aside.

Her voice faded out and for a bit they sat together, merely staring into the leap of the fire. She bent toward him, suddenly, to look closely into his face. "Steve?" She touched his hand. When he turned to look at her, she smiled, her face inches from his and the tree candles shining in her eyes. "Thank goodness! I thought maybe I'd put you to sleep with my jabber."

"Please don't stop!" On an impulse he seized her hand and she let it slide confidently into his. "If you had any idea how nice it is to listen to you, how long it's been since I've heard anything that sounded half as good!"

"Poor Steve!" She shook her head in sympathy.

He lifted a hand idly to touch one of the ash-blond curls that lay against her throat. "You're a sweet kid, Bobby. . . ." Not really thinking, he let his fingers move to rest upon the skin of her neck.

It was warm, and satin-smooth, and faintly troubling. He saw her take a quick breath, and her smile became a little uncertain; but in her trusting confidence in him she did not move away from his touch.

Some corner of his mind warned him: *Stop* this. . . .

Instead, contented and drowsy and off guard in the fire's warmth and candle glow, he ran his fingers idly along the line of her neck to the shoulder. He felt her tremble against him. He kissed her on the throat, and his arms were suddenly hard about her.

He neither knew nor cared if she returned his kiss. Passion was on him and it hardly mattered who this was in his arms.

Suddenly, revulsion shook him, brought him stumbling to his feet as the girl fell back upon the cushions. He stood looking at her and his hands worked, fingers opening and closing. "I'm sorry, Bobby!" he blurted hoarsely. "I am! Honest to God I am!"

When she said nothing, merely looked at him in bewilderment and the beginning of shame, he went on bitterly, "You'll never believe again I have any respect for you — but I have! It's just that I —"

He swung away, and the thick envelope in his coat pocket brushed a sleeve. Plucking it forth, he turned and dropped Ed Loman's letter in her lap. "I nearly forgot this. Maybe, if I'd only remembered it sooner —"

With a shrug he strode out of the room. He jerked hat and coat from the peg by the door, let the heavy panel slam behind him. On the steps he stood, and the cold wind washed against him.

Overhead, stars burned and were mirrored in the lamps of Nebraska City, lying below this high bluff along the ice-clogged river. His horse still drooped its head at the hitching post where he had tied it.

Why had he, like a fool, not taken what had been right in his grasp? And at once, unwillingly, he admitted that he knew the answer. Not fear of Martin Wilcox, certainly. Not even — or not entirely — any latent respect for innocence, or for young Loman, who was his friend and Bobby's sweetheart. No, what had checked him had a deeper source, a truth about himself which, he realized, he had tried not to see but which he could no longer deny.

It was the ghost of Melissa; while she lived in his heart there could not be for him any other woman, not without this guilty feeling of betrayal. Not even knowing, as he knew in all its finality, that she belonged forever to another.

He walked heavily down the steps, and

untied the reins. For a long moment he stood with head bowed, looking at the snow his horse's hoofs had trampled in its waiting. He shook his head, and said aloud, "It looks like we're stuck, all right, pony!"

Knowing what he knew, there could be but one object for him now. He still had his obligations to Martin Wilcox, and the men marooned out on the snow-held wastes of the Plains; but even above this job, his purpose must be somehow to find a peaceful ending to the trouble between Saint and Gentile, to avert the disaster that threatened the happiness of Melissa and the man she had chosen.

A tall order — and a bitter assignment for a man to hand himself!

# 14

Late spring had come to this land before Steve Corey was able to head west again. It had been a hectic winter, a man-killing time when each day brought its decisions and its pressuring needs. Somehow he had done the impossible, scraping together more wagons, more livestock, more men. Somehow — without stretching Wilcox's thinning resources to the breaking point — he had managed to put new trains together. Almost before the drifts were gone and a bottom formed beneath the hub-deep morass of the prairie trails, he had thrown the trains on the road, their orders to get supplies through somehow to the expedition marooned at Camp Scott.

And as soon as it was humanly possible for him to leave, he'd thrown the saddle on his pony and set out himself.

The roads were as yet scarcely passable; Fort Kearney on the Platte lay in a sea of viscid mud torn by hoofs and wheels. As Corey brought his train of twenty big wagons to a corral, sunset colors were being swallowed by black clouds that promised still more washout rains, more mud and slop.

Even though the road from Nebraska City was largely free of swollen streams such as plagued traffic along the old Fort Leavenworth route, fighting the greasy trails had already told on men and teams alike. They were far behind schedule, yet Corey had to order a layover here to rest the sorely used oxen, and make repairs. These were not the brand-new, blue-and-red Espenshieds that had rolled west, last year, to face a disastrous winter campaign. New wagons, ordered for spring, were as yet undelivered, and in order to equip his relief trains Steve had been forced to take anything at all that he could find in the emergency.

Some of these wagons were battered relics of the Santa Fe trade; in addition to their loads they had to carry a generous weight of spare timbers lashed beneath the boxes for road repairs when they broke down — as they were always doing. It being the last safe layover before the long, tilting haul along the Platte to Laramie fort, Steve had to allow two full days here while every timber had its careful check for weaknesses, and the loads were repacked.

At the fort, he inquired after any news that might have come from the West, news of Johnston's army, and the situation in Utah. He could learn little. He took this silence to mean that things remained at a standstill; out there at winter quarters, the higher altitude would mean the season was less far advanced; the army would not yet have recovered from its recent disasters and be ready to take the field again. But weeks would pass before this slow-moving train could reach Camp Scott, and this thought filled Corey with a deep impatience.

It was late afternoon of the second day, when a man rode up forking a ratty-looking roan mare without a saddle—scarecrow figures, rider and horse alike. The derelict pulled in and ran a bony wrist across his nose, red and running with a cold. His voice held a rheumy whine. "Your name Corey?"

Steve was dismounted, checking one of his horse's front hoofs for signs of lameness. He straightened, slowly. At his curt nod the stranger added, meaningly, "I heard you was looking for a man. A redhead."

"Where did you hear a thing like that?"

The derelict lifted gaunt shoulders.

"Word gits around — you know how it is. Way I had it, you wanted to see this Bill Reno, awful bad."

"So — ?"

"I could lead you right to him," the man said. "If you was to make it worth my while, of course — I don't enjoy monkeying with no killer like Reno."

Steve Corey studied him for a long moment. The outside chance that this man might actually help him lay hands on the murderer of Ole Jorgesen finally swayed the balance.

"All right," he said curtly. "You'll have to show me, first."

"Sure." The tramp added eagerly, chapped lips parting in a grin. "I trust you. Won't need but a few minutes of your time."

Steve located his second-in-command, and gave him instructions to take over. Something must have showed in his face, to judge from the careful, keen scrutiny he got; but the wagonman asked no questions. Steve knew he was watched as he rode off across the hock-deep mud with his disreputable guide.

Corey was not much surprised to see that they were heading for Dobeytown. The squalid mushroom growth of saloons

224

and cribs and gambling dens that had sprung up at the edge of the military reservation was the obvious place to look for a man like Bill Reno. He rode with sharp attention as they threaded their way past clustered tipis of friendly blanket Indians, and then through thickening shadows into a ragged scatter of sod huts and log buildings.

A woman leaning in a dimly lighted doorway called out to him, and then cursed as he rode on. A couple of troopers from the nearby fort, drunk already this early in the evening, stumbled in front of the sorrel's nose. This was still too early in the season for Dobeytown to be at its peak. Later on, the summer nights would find its cribs and deadfalls crowded with bullwhackers and emigrants, soldiers and mountain men; but now the muddy streets were nearly empty. Darkness settled, broken by the few lamps burning inside the dingy buildings, softening their ugly contours but investing them with an evil quality.

The saloon his guide led him to was a dingy affair of mud-chinked logs, shakeroofed. Not much light leaked through its single window of oiled paper, but the door was propped wide open. The bar was opposite; a man stood leaning against it, under the spray of yellow light from a lamp which burned in a bracket on the wall. Steve Corey had no trouble recognizing the gangling length and hunched shoulders and the shine of reddish hair that hung across the collar of Bill Reno's patched leather shirt.

He nodded shortly. "All right," he said. "You told it straight, I guess."

Digging into a pocket, he brought out a handful of silver dollars. The derelict's fingers clutched the money. He mumbled something, and kicked his ribby mount with his heels. Corey watched him until the shadows swallowed him and the sucking sounds of the horse's hoofs in the muck of the street faded.

After that he turned his attention back to the open doorway of the saloon, while he slowly dismounted. The man at the bar lifted a tin cup and drank, his head jerking back as he spilled the cheap "pilgrim whisky." Corey shuddered a little, thinking of the potency of that man-killing stuff — whole-grain alcohol, flavored with gunpowder and plug tobacco and other unmentionable ingredients. Reno set the cup down and wiped his mouth on a sleeve.

There was no one on duty behind the

crude, pine-plank bar. Reno seemed to be entirely alone.

Corey thought of Ole Jorgesen lying dead in the snow, clothing stiff and black with blood from a knife-thrust between his shoulders He let a hand touch the cap-and-ball Navy and loosen it in the holster. Puncheons, warped and uneven, echoed to the stride of his boots as he walked directly to the bar, and placed himself a little distance at the right of Reno.

The man did not move, or look at him. He stood with both elbows on the bar, bearded head sunk forward. He appeared to have been knocked into a stupor by the liquor he had drunk. But then, looking at him more closely, Corey felt a sudden, warning stir of the short hairs at the back of his neck.

Though Reno had showed no awareness of him, Steve knew all at once that he was not drunk at all — that actually he stood tensed and waiting. His dirty hands were clamped tightly upon the edge of the bar, so that the knuckles showed white beneath stretched skin. And on the high cheekbone there was the faintest sheen of moisture.

It was not a warm enough evening to cause any man to sweat.

Too late, Corey pivoted, and his hand

jerked downward. He did not touch the holstered gun. Just to the left of the open door, shoulders against the logs and a revolver leveled, Jud Noonan was ready for him. Jud said only one word: "No!"

It was enough; his face puckered in a grin of vindictive pleasure as he saw Corey hesitate. And now Bill Reno had lifted his head and he too was grinning. Corey looked into the narrow face, with its ragged growth of beard and the scar tissue of some forgotten knife-cut gleaming through the rusty stubble.

Off in the dimness the sudden scrape of a chair shifted his glance, and with an unpleasant start of surprise he saw York Baggett seated at a card table, a whisky jug in front of him. Though Baggett did not smile, there was an air of unveiled satisfaction about him as he drummed the table top with nervous fingers and returned Steve Corey's stare.

Jud Noonan gave the order: "Take your gun out of the holster, and lay it on the bar. Do it slow."

There was nothing to do but comply. A sick futility roiled in him, seeing that room now as he should have in the beginning — the single lamp burning, the barkeeper bribed and out of the way, Reno waiting alone in full view of the street. "So you had it all set up for me! I must be getting old, to walk into a trap like this one."

York Baggett told him, "We rather thought Reno could decoy you into it, if anything could."

"My mistake," said Steve, bitterly, "was in not finishing him off a long time ago. If I had, Ole Jorgesen would be alive today." He turned back to the redhead. "Why did you kill him, Reno?"

The shoulders inside the leather shirt lifted. "Personal matter."

"Was it? Or did he get in the way too much? Can't Jud Noonan manage his own killings?"

That brought a savage oath from the man by the door, but York Baggett cut it off. Rising, Baggett said, "We'll forget about Jorgesen!" He took his hat and, leaving the whisky jug, came over to the bar, into the weak yellow gleam of the single wall lamp. He drew the hat on, settled his box coat upon his shoulders. There was a scurf of unshaven whiskers on his face, and it struck Corey that his jowls had actually softened and sagged a little; every time he laid eyes on this man, it seemed, the process of deterioration had gone noticeably forward. But the spiteful gleam in his eyes was sharp as ever.

"When it comes to getting in the way," he said, "you could give anyone aces and spades! You've made trouble from the start, Corey; after that evening in Nebraska City, I knew it could only be a matter of time before I had to get rid of you. Well, the time is now!" He looked at Noonan. "I turn him over to you two. I'll hold you responsible for a good job."

Jud Noonan's teeth showed as he grinned. "You don't need to worry!"

"I'll be at the fort. Let me know when the thing is done — but be careful. We can't have anyone tracing it to me!"

He stepped through the door without another look at the doomed man. And it struck Corey that this moment was the likeliest chance he would have: for though they meant to kill him, their minds were set to the idea of waiting until Baggett was gone. As it was, he faced a gun in Jud Noonan's hand; and Reno was fingering the haft of the knife in his belt sheath. Steve's gun lay there, at Reno's elbow, just out of reach.

Steve chose Bill Reno and made his lunge with a balled fist swinging.

A cry of warning broke from Jud Noonan, but Steve had moved in on Reno too fast for him to shoot. The one chance was to keep crowding, confusing his enemies until he could reach that gun upon the counter. His fist caught the redhead high on the chest and drove him back. Steve was watching that right elbow; now he saw it jerk, knew that Reno was bringing out his knife even before the blade flashed lamplight. He bore in, desperately, groping to trap the hand that held the knife.

To grapple, unarmed, against that blade was like trying to stay the strike of a snake. Moving fast, Steve lashed a right fist into Reno's bearded jaw. At the same moment, he felt the tug of the knifepoint rip his clothing.

Fiery pain sprang, like a lightning stroke, through his belly. Stumbling away, he felt the hard edge of the bar strike his back. He stared numbly at blood reddening the front of his clothing; lifted his head and saw Reno waiting, at a crouch, the knife poised. He heard the harsh scrape of his own breathing, saw Reno shake his head at Jud Noonan, and heard Noonan's gun click to full cock in the room's stillness.

"He's mine!" Reno grunted. Noonan slowly lowered the weapon.

As the first shock of the knife-cut passed,

Corey realized dimly that it had done no more harm than to slice across his ribs. He was bleeding freely, and a burning, throbbing pain was thawing out the numbness in his side, but the ugly blade had not actually cut deep.

Slowly he pushed himself erect, a steadying hand on the edge of the wood. At once, Bill Reno dropped into a crouch. Reno must have caught the brief shifting of Steve's glance toward the gun that lay on the counter; he put out a hand and gave it a shove that toppled it to the floor behind the bar.

"Come ahead," he said, softly. "Walk right over and get it!" When Corey made no move he started forward himself, along the bar, the bloodied point leveled and ready.

Steve let him come. Then, at the precise, timed instant, with a hand braced against the bar, he swung his left leg — hard. The toe of the muddy boot struck Reno's arm, and before either of his enemies could recover from surprise, Steve lunged. Noonan's shout was in his ears, but Jud could not use his gun. With Reno's body shielding his own, Steve brought the captured arm down across the point of his hip, a chopping blow. Reno screamed in pain and the knife clattered out of his hand, onto the floor.

But now Steve could no longer hold him, for Reno's threshing drove an elbow into his knife-cut ribs. In the moment of agony his arms seemed to lose all their strength. Jerking away, Reno hurled him to one knee. And just then a gun fired.

The bullet drilled into the bar's facing only inches off its hasty target.

Corey was off the floor and after Reno before Jud Noonan could shoot again. Without a knife, Reno was no fighter. Steve knocked his defense aside, and his hands closed on the man's filthy buckskin shirt. He whirled, literally throwing the man at Noonan, as Noonan fired.

Reno's body jerked; lifeless, he fell against Noonan and drove the man back a pace. Corey was already turning toward the bar. He went around behind it, saw his own gun on the floor, and knelt to grab it up. His hand was slick with blood, the whole front of his body soaked. Dizziness went through him. He shook his head to clear it; then, slanting a look up, saw the single oil lamp burning on the wall above his head. He raised the gun, and fired. Glass and burning oil showered around him, and the room plunged into total darkness.

He waited, gunbarrel laid across the wood, letting his eyes become adjusted; yonder the open door took shape, a square of darkness only faintly less dense than the black velvet of the room.

Now Jud Noonan's gun hammered out a couple of quick shots. Steve threw bullet at the flashes, and then sidestepped hastily, but there was no answer. Instead, boots sloughed noisily on the puncheons, and all at once he saw Jud Noonan's dark shape briefly, as he plunged out the door.

Noonan lacked courage to face another gun, in a darkened room. The fight was over.

Suddenly shaky, Steve laid his gun upon the bar and fumbled at the knife-cut along his ribs, on the left side. He was still bleeding like a stuck pig, but it wasn't bad enough to put him down.

Jud Noonan would be on his way to find York Baggett and warn him how things had gone wrong. But Jud would have to beat Corey to him!

Grim with purpose, Steve picked up the smoking gun. He circled around the bar, began moving across the darkened room toward the door. Outside he could hear shouting and the running of men converging on the scene of disturbance. Then, abruptly, the sounds blurred and everything darkened inside him, and he fell. . . .

When he awoke, in broad daylight, he was on a makeshift bed made up in the back of one of his own freight wagons, rolling west from Kearney. His crew had found him and bandaged him as best they could; he started up, remembering his incompleted business with York Baggett, but firm hands pushed him down and would not let him rise. And after that a drained weakness held him, powerless.

# 15

Camp Scott showed many signs of the ordeal the Utah Expedition had undergone, wintering in this improvised encampment. Despite the protecting rise of the bluff behind it, the row on row of Sibley tents were weather-stained and battered. The infantrymen that Corey saw as he rode his horse through the place had the gaunted, stare-eyed look of men defeated by cold and by months of near-starvation. Even though new life was being pumped into this army now with the arrival of the relief trains, most still wore the filthy rags of their worn-out and ruined uniforms. There scarcely seemed to be a sound overcoat or pair of boots in the camp.

Steve Corey rode into the camp holding himself a little stiffly, though the knife wound had largely healed during the time of the crossing. York Baggett, he knew, was likely to be somewhere around, and Steve found himself watching for any sign of him; but it was not Baggett or Jud Noonan either, that he sought just now.

This was not a time for personal settlements.

A plan had taken form in his mind, during the slow days of convalescing in the back of that jolting freight wagon; a last, desperate resort, born of the knowledge that only cool daring and personal risk could avert a bloody war — and that he perhaps was the one man who could hope to do it.

He asked instructions from the first trooper he encountered slogging along a bottomless company street; being directed to the far end of the camp, he nodded his thanks and rode that way. Headquarters consisted of a cluster of dugouts, unpeeled-log and brush-roof structures built above holes in the ground; here the civil officials of the Territory of Utah had spent the winter. Further inquiry found him the particular hut he sought. Smoke rose above a vent hole in the roof. Steve dismounted and hammered on the soddie's plank door.

Governor Alfred Cumming, himself, opened it.

The governor said, in surprise, "Corey!" He stepped back to let his visitor enter. He looked like a ghost of himself, his portly figure so wasted that the clothes hung on him. The room, which the governor shared with three other men, was a depressing place of the crudest makeshift furnishings. Steve looked around and wondered how a man like Cumming could have endured this. But the governor looked to be in good spirits, and somehow he managed to appear almost as well and neatly dressed as when Corey first saw him, in Johnston's office in Laramie.

The two of them were, at the moment, the room's only occupants. Cumming's shrewd glance studied over the other man. "I'd say you had been traveling," he remarked. "You also look as though you'd just got over a sickness."

"I have," Corey briefly answered both conjectures. He unhooked the buttons of his heavy coat and threw it back, against the warmth of the blaze in a small iron stove. "We hit camp only a half hour ago."

"And you came directly to me." Cumming's look held all his curiosity.

Steve had taken a couple of cigars from a pocket and offered one to the governor; he saw the almost reverent delight as the other took it, breathed its aroma and closed his eyes. "Man, if you only knew! I even came to the point of trying some of Cal Finney's kinnikinnick!"

"How was it — pretty good?" Steve

asked with dry humor, and grinned at the face the other made. The ice broken by this offering of good tobacco, they lit up in silence; the governor took the first puffs deeply. But his eyes were serious as he said quickly, "Something's on your mind, Corey."

Steve nodded. "I wanted to talk to you, about — all of this." His gesture indicated the squalid dugout, the camp that spread around them in the April mud. "How has it been?"

Cumming shrugged. "Rugged, I believe the word is. I never should have thought I had it in me to pioneer, but after that winter I'll know I'm made of sterner stuff than I imagined. Helpful for the waistline, too." He patted his middle, which had lost inches of its former girth, and smiled in good-natured mockery at himself. But then his manner turned sober. "It was very bad," he finished, quietly. "We're fortunate to have got through."

"Were there any dead?" Corey demanded.

"What would you expect, with malnutrition and exposure and not enough of anything? There were times when we had so many on the sick rolls that a good strong force of Mormons could have wiped us out, if they'd been minded to attack. But what of that?" he added, with a shrug. "It's past, and we have to look to the future."

"And, the general?"

"Fit, and ready to move ahead with the campaign."

"I was afraid of that!"

His tone brought him the governor's narrowed regard. Cumming said, "I'm wondering what you mean."

Puffing at his cigar, Steve Corey took a pace or two across the beaten dirt of the dugout's floor, debating the argument he had been framing in his mind over the weary miles west. "Governor Cumming," he said suddenly, putting his glance on the man, "wouldn't you like to see this thing settled without coming to a lot of bloodshed?"

"Certainly. But haven't things gone too far to hope for that? The Mormons showed open defiance by their actions last winter. They've treated the United States Army with complete contempt. Brigham Young found out somehow the camp was short of salt and he sent a couple of men out with a wagon-load, as a gift — but their very manner was an insult and General Johnston refused."

"That seems foolish! The troops could have used salt."

Cumming lifted a shoulder. "The Saints went away and left the wagon sitting just outside camp. The troops had their salt, all right. But," he went on, "Johnston is a proud man — and his pride has been stung by the humiliating way this expedition was stopped in its tracks, by weather and a mere handful of militia. Now I'm afraid his mind is pretty much set on revenge, and he has the Administration behind him."

"That could change," said Steve, crisply. From a pocket he took a folded strip of newsprint. "Take a look at this editorial. I cut it out of the Kansas City paper, just before I left."

"You hear the same sentiments wherever you turn, back there," he said when Cumming had finished reading. "Nobody puts any blame on Johnston for the way the campaign has developed. But they are beginning to raise questions about a policy that ties up the cream of the army and thousands of dollars worth of supplies here in the wilderness, to no clear purpose except to fill the pockets of a few contractors like York Baggett.

"People have had time to cool off on this Mormon controversy," he went on, sensing that he held the governor's close attention. "They think the Saints should be given a fair chance to air their side. In fact, do you want to know what this campaign is being labeled, back East? They're calling it 'Buchanan's Blunder'!"

The governor seemed to consider closely what Steve had told him. His eyes puckered suddenly in a frown. "And what about the Mountain Meadow massacre?" he demanded sharply. "Have they forgotten that? Are they ready to write it off as a harmless sort of prank?"

"They think Brigham should be allowed to explain — to prove, if he can, that the Church wasn't involved. And I agree."

"And so you came to me." Cumming shook his head. "Don't you know I haven't the power to call off this campaign? Even if I did have that kind of influence in Washington, there'd be no time. Johnston is ready to march!"

"I know that. There's just one thing that might have results: a conference, between you and Brigham Young!"

He thought Cumming was going to scoff; instead the man's brow creased thoughtfully. He said only, "Go ahead."

"I know Brigham," Steve explained. "I probably know at least a few of the men guarding Echo Canyon. If we were to go under a flag of truce, my thought is they might let us in. Maybe not. Maybe every Mormon figures me a traitor after the way I've helped their enemies — and I'm beginning to think they could be right. Just the same, face to face with Young there's at least a hope of working out something. Otherwise I don't see anything now to avert a bloody war."

Head bowed as be considered, Cumming turned and walked slowly to the stove; he raised the lid a moment to check the fire within. Puffing furiously on his cigar, he turned back and lifted a carefully polished, high-topped shoe onto an empty ammunition box that served the dugout for a chair. He leaned a forearm on his bent knee. "How large an escort?"

"Just you and me would be best."

"You and me." Cumming tilted his head, spearing him with a searching look. "And your sole interest is a love of justice? I don't know, Corey. The whole thing sounds risky."

Steve's anger, simmering slowly under all this argument and close questioning, suddenly broke out. "All right, Governor!" he snapped. "I wanted to make the suggestion. If you're afraid to tackle it, I won't push you."

With a curt nod he turned and put his

hand on the door to throw it open. Cumming's mild words, holding no rancor, brought him around again.

"I suppose you can scare up an extra horse. And trail rations —"

"Then you'll go with me?" Steve took a deep breath, savoring this one small triumph. "Be ready to ride. It's a long distance, and I hope we can make Echo Canyon before dark. We want the guards to be able to see a flag of truce."

"I'll be ready by the time you bring that horse."

Steve was tired enough from the trail, but he took new energy from the success of his appeal to the governor. Impatient now to be riding, he went seeking a spare mount at the place where the wagons he had brought with him were being emptied of their cargo. Here he found Ed Loman, working with a bunch of men to check a wagon manifest against the unloaded goods.

Steve called his friend's name and quickly reined over. His voice carried above the hubbub of the place; Ed heard, looked around. His face was utterly without expression. When Steve spoke again, only some five yards from him, Loman all at once shoved the wagon papers into the hand of one of his helpers and started to walk away.

Anger and alarm struck through Corey as he watched Ed stride at a swift pace through the confusion of men and wagons, boxes, tents. He spurred forward and black mire sucked at the horse's hoofs as he came from behind to overtake the man; he knew young Loman heard him approach, but with head held stiffly and shoulders straight he refused to look around, even when Steve called his name a third time.

Exasperated, Corey jumped the horse ahead and pulled it around sharp, cutting in front and forcing the other to a halt against the muddy canvas of a tent that shut off further retreat. Ed faced him with hands clenched and with mouth pinched and tight at the corners, his whole face made white by some unnamed emotion.

Quickly Steve stepped down into the mud. "What's the matter with you?" he demanded.

He saw his friend's mouth work with rage that caused his lips and whole lower jaw to tremble. Then it came out, blurted and almost incoherent: "She wrote me — !"

So that was the shape of it! There was suddenly nothing to say, for he understood the trouble and had no possible answer or defense. But Ed Loman was just beginning, and Steve could sense the torment that welled behind his blazing eyes, came through his lips in a rush of furious speech:

"A damned tomcat! I didn't know you were like that — not you, Corey! — not till what I saw that time at the handcart camp. Of course, that didn't matter; she was nothing but a Mormon, anyway. But when you dare to lay your filthy paws on Bobby Wilcox —"

"All right, Ed," grunted Steve, tiredly, merely trying to stem the spate of words before the real ugliness came; and he turned away. At once Ed's hand seized his shoulder, whirling him, and Ed's right fist smashed him a glancing blow that raked along the side of his jaw.

His boots slipped in the mud and he almost went down, a stab of pain wrenching his hurt side, but he reached for Ed. It was an instinctive action, unleashed by the sting of the blow. He grabbed a tight fistful of the man's clothing and held him, while his arm cocked for retaliation. But Steve checked himself and they stood like that a moment, with Ed's furious eyes staring straight into his and Ed's chest swelling to his harsh breathing. Steve found himself trying to speak, but after all there was nothing to say.

He sighed, and shook his head. Letting go of Ed, then, he shoved the man from him, against the tent. Loman grabbed a stake rope to balance himself. Not looking back, Steve Corey caught up his reins and swung himself to the saddle. When he rode away, he knew Ed Loman was still clinging to the tent rope — watching him go, and hating him with everything in his being.

After the first mile or two, Corey and the governor spoke seldom; there was little to say now that the decision had been taken and they were launched on this dubious course. Steve, conscious at the passing of the time and the sun's inexorable approach to the dark mountains ahead, set a pace that the other man, less hardened to saddle work, could meet only by putting all his strength into the effort.

So they rode in silence, across a bleak land of empty sage hills where grass and scrubby brush were greening now, and where wild geese speared the pale sky and were noisy on the shallows of the streams.

Anxious as he was to beat out the waning of daylight, Steve barely condescended to pause long enough to rest the tiring horses, and to dig out cold rations for himself and his companion. As they ate he looked at Cumming and noticed for the first time how the ordeal was telling on the man. But Cumming made no complaint and asked for no easing of the pace, and Steve was not in any mood to make allowances for the discomforts of tired bodies, or the dull ache of a half-healed knife wound.

The sun, slipping westward toward the jagged bulk of the Wasatch Range, told him they had already lost this race. Still, they pushed on, topping at last the treeless crest of a divide. With dusk lying like water about them and a lemon-yellow afterglow showing above the peaks of the wail that held the Basin, they saw the beginning of Echo Canyon, dead ahead.

Involuntarily they drew rein. In the clear air of this high country, bare red rock seemed to swim with gathered shadow. There was no sound or movement, only the blowing of their tired horses, the popping of leather as the governor shifted in his saddle, uneasily.

"Do we go on?"

"They've undoubtedly spotted us," Steve Corey pointed out. Lashed to his saddle was a length of tree limb that he had picked up along the trail, and he proceeded methodically to take this down and tie to one end of it the white square of cloth he had brought for the purpose. There were any number of places where a sharpshooter could rest the barrel of his long gun and notch his sights on the chest of a nearing rider. The thought was enough to trace a chill on a man's backbone, and start a sweat upon him.

Steve shook out his crude flag of truce, raised it and set the butt of the limb against his thigh. The wind caught the cloth and snapped it above his head. He said, "I didn't come this far just to sit here all night, expecting them to sneak out any minute and grab me off. Let's ride ahead!"

Cumming nodded, accepting his decision without argument.

The way began to roughen; their descent was rapid as they followed the creek that had carved this way through native rock. Bare red walls began to lift on either side, the lower reaches spotted with willow and aspen and a few scrubby cedars. Down here the day's last light gleamed faintly from saddle trappings, and found the white flutter of the stick-tied cloth raised in Corey's hand. The slow, ragged beat of their horses' hoofs bounced away, oddly magnified and repeated by the sheer surfaces of the canyon wall.

Because of the echoes, the shouted challenge when it finally came seemed to leap at them from a dozen different directions. Uncertain and contused, both halted. At the sudden pull of the reins the horse under Corey stepped sideways and tossed its head nervously; he calmed it with a word. Again the voice spoke, and this time sounded very close, though they still could not locate its source.

"Keep your hands clear! We've got a dozen guns trained on you."

Steve Corey lifted an angry answer. "Doesn't this flag mean anything?"

"It probably means a trick!"

"How could it?" he retorted. "We're alone — you can tell that!"

The echoes of his voice chased themselves away, along the reaches of the canyon side; again silence fell. Steve could feel the itchy sting of sweat crawling down across his ribs.

Then, without warning, a half-dozen men were melting out of the shadows. Steve's hand made an involuntary move in the direction of his gun, but he checked it; even in the dimming light he could see that other weapons had him ringed. He glanced at his companion. Cumming's face was expressionless, the jaw firmly clamped.

"Who's in command here?" Corey demanded. "Would I have ridden under a flag if my aims weren't peaceful? Let me talk to somebody in charge."

Someone retorted, angrily, "Who's givin' orders?" But before he could reply, a new man, this one mounted, rode up and the rest fell silent He brought his horse to a halt facing the strangers. "What is this?" he demanded.

Steve repeated his request, and saw only suspicion in the man's face as he listened. "Your names?" he said then, sharply.

"Mine's Steve Corey. And this is Albert Cumming — your new governor."

There was a quick reaction. Steve heard the startled murmur that ran through the group, and he saw the astonished look on his questioner give way to one of hard satisfaction. "Delivered right into our hands! Well, that's real considerate, mister!"

Slowly, then, the governor turned his head and his eyes sought Corey's; in them was a newly born and terrible suspicion. Steve felt a cold knotting in his belly, and he retorted angrily: "Don't be a fool! It'll be more than your life is worth if you dare to lay a hand on him!" He added, "If you've got the authority to let us through the canyon, then I'll talk to you. If not, please take us to someone who has."

The others seemed to consider, while the rest of the Mormons waited. Then, as though his mind was made up, the leader kneed his horse closer and pointed to the gun at Corey's waist. "I'll have to take those, first."

It was a ticklish matter, but they were in too deep to have a choice. Without a word, Corey tossed aside his truce flag and, slipping the weapon from holster, passed it over. The governor was slower to obey; afterward, when they were both disarmed, the leader pulled back and a jerk of the head motioned them forward. As they moved, they heard him tell his men: "Keep your eyes peeled for trouble — I don't trust any Gentile!"

He spurred to catch up with the prisoners, indicating a trail that led off through the brush to their left. "That way," he ordered, and Steve knew then where they were being taken.

The governor had said nothing at all, as yet. From his manner Corey knew that he was plagued by doubts of the wisdom of this thing they had undertaken.

The cave was a black hole in the canyon

wall, its entrance the height of a man on the back of a horse. A fire blazed in front of it, combating the chill of newly settled darkness, and within there was the glow of lanterns. Their guide gave a hail and, as they rode up, a tall, spare figure stepped out into the fireglow; Corey, seeing the gaunt shape of the man, suddenly recognized him and knew a deep, inward swelling of relief.

"Steve Corey!" Eli Bishnell had known him in the same instant. "What in the world — !"

"How are you, Eli?" Steve swung down tiredly from the saddle, and gave his hand to the other's grasp. "I hardly expected to run into *you* here, but there's no one I'd rather see!" He introduced his companion then.

This man with whom he had worked for a year establishing the B. Y. Express turned cautious. "What do you want?" he demanded.

Steve said, "I've given the governor my personal assurance that you people will let us through unharmed, for a talk with Brigham Young — if Brigham will see us!"

The Mormon frowned. "You had no authority to make that kind of promise!"

"I had to make it! It's the last chance for

peace. Don't you realize," he insisted, "there's an army at Fort Bridger, and another in reserve at Leavenworth? There's the whole power of the nation, to blast a way through this canyon and take the Basin by force, if you make it come to that! You're only a handful; you can't hope to stand against it. But let us through now — just the two of us — and there's a chance a parley between Brigham and the governor can reach a settlement."

The man who had brought them said, heavily, "How do we know this ain't a trick?"

"How could it be?" Steve retorted, turning on him. "We're in your hands. You can do what you want with us!"

Governor Cumming spoke up, for the first time. "Corey has told it to you exactly. I risked letting him bring me here because he assured me you were reasonable men, who would welcome a chance to iron out our differences. I think I've shown I'm willing to do anything in my power. It's up to you, now, to meet me half way!"

There was a silence. They watched Eli Bishnell turn away and walk, head down in thought, to stand looking into the fire. The Mormon leader bent and picked up a length of cottonwood and dropped it in, and the wood crackled and the sparks leaped upward.

He came back to them, then, and his decision was not readable in his eyes. What he said was, "You didn't want to go on tonight, did you?"

A deep breath swelled Corey's lungs, as he saw that he had won. He exchanged a look with Cumming. The governor was gray with fatigue, and Steve's own body was leaden and aching from the knife wound. But he told the Mormon, "We're in a hurry; time is getting short. We need fresh horses, though."

"Get them," Bishnell told the other man, and the latter nodded and rode into the darkness. And Eli Bishnell told the two, "I'll make out a pass, and see that it's honored. I don't know what, if anything, you'll be able to accomplish; but I wish you both luck! No one wants to see this thing settled more than I do. I'm not looking forward to the moment when that army hits our defenses, here in Echo Canyon."

With fresh mounts under them, and their Mormon escort surly at their backs, they rode deeper into the narrow gut of darkness. Full night had come, the stars peppered the stretch of sky overhead and the creek seemed to run more loudly. They had to cross it, time and again. The darkness was not complete, for they discovered their way was lighted at intervals by the brush fires of the Mormon garrison. These specks of brightness took shape ahead of them, drew slowly abreast until they could see the shadows of men moving about the fires, then dwindled again at their rear; and so they rode steadily on, accompanied by the echo of their own progress bouncing back off the high lifts of red rock.

Once, their escort called to them, "Take a look up there to your right." Obeying, they saw the heaped-up shadow of rock, above the overhanging rim. "A shove would be enough to send those boulders down. We got 'em piled like that all along the walls of this canyon. We got sharpshooters spotted behind parapets. And over at the west end — just supposing they should break through us — there's ditches dug and dams built that will flood the trails. Believe me, we haven't wasted our time this winter. We're set and ready!"

Steve Corey answered him: "It's no good. There's too many of them; you'd never hold them back, once they started through!"

The man grunted and was silent; but

Steve thought his words were sinking in.

The night, and the fireglow, and the monotonous pacing of the horses had a soporific effect, but danger helped to keep him alert. Once or twice they were challenged, but the escort was there to answer and make the necessary explanations. The moon threw silver across the brush that clung to the canyon's sloping south wall, though here at the base of the other, steeper side was only darkness. High above their heads, swallows, disturbed by the flickering dance of the campfires, darted silently among the shadows where their nests were hung.

It was near midnight when they reached the Narrows; here, where the walls pinched in, a breastworks had been constructed, and here was a large-sized camp, with crude structures made of brush and saplings and long wheat grass; this, seemingly was to be the place of last-ditch defense. And at this point the riders found themselves quickly surrounded.

Steve caught the governor's eye and shook his head, signaling Cumming to keep quiet and let their escort handle the argument if there was to be one. They were left with a half-dozen guns to cover them while Eli Bishnell's pass was presented and a discussion went on beside the fire; for a long and sweaty moment the matter seemed to be touch and go.

Then the guard came striding back, took his reins from the man who held them, and swung into the saddle with a jerk of his head at the two Gentiles. They put their horses after his, and a few hundred yards farther on their guide drew rein to face them.

Steve found his pistol thrust toward him, butt first. "The way is clear, from here," the Mormon told them. He added, grudgingly, "I wish you luck with Brigham!"

"Thanks," Steve answered. He lifted his hand in salute. The man nodded and reined aside; tiredly, the two men kicked their horses forward.

The last obstacle was behind them. Ahead the trail lay open, into the great Basin of the Saints.

# 16

Along Weber River cottonwoods were green with spring; the red soil wore its new carpeting of grass; the brush had the live blush of fresh leaf. They broke camp early, riding west and south, and presently, at their right hand, the vast spread of the lake itself showed leaden-gray under mid-morning sunlight, and the quartering breeze brought to them the stinging smell of salt.

They saw a deserted land of empty villages. They rode through streets where houses stared at them with sightless windows, and only the sound of their own passage broke the stillness. Once Steve asked drily, "Well, are you convinced they meant what they said about taking to the hills?"

The other man looked troubled. "Where have they gone?"

Corey jerked his head southward.

"I thought they spoke about burning everything."

"Not an easy thing to do, Governor, not even for a people as stubborn as the Saints. But they'll have left a rear guard. If an army comes, they'll apply the torches!"

"What will we find at Salt Lake City?" the governor exclaimed.

What they found, when they rode into it in midafternoon, was an eerie and silent place — a city lying dead. There were still people here, but most were gone; and Corey pointed out what the other man had already noticed himself: the heaps of baled straw and tinder, carefully piled against the empty buildings. All that was needed was a match.

"The first alarm," Steve said, "and they touch it off."

Cumming could only shake his head. "I didn't know there were such people!"

"Let's hope we find Brigham," Corey reminded him, "and that he'll listen to us."

Temple Square looked as deserted as the rest of the city. The Lion House with its tall, gray chimneys, and its many gabled windows, each marking the apartment of one of Brigham's wives, had that indefinable air of a building whose occupants have fled. But Steve had a conviction that Brigham Young himself would be among the last to leave the city; and so, with little hesitation, he swung down before the smaller office building next door, and Cumming followed. With his hand lifted,

Corey hesitated briefly, struck by last-minute doubts. But then he knocked, and after a moment the door was opened by the very man they had made this long ride to see.

A strange man, of indomitable will and vision that bordered on the flamboyant, this leader of all the Mormon people greeted them in a chill silence that was not promising. He heard Corey's introduction of the Gentile who had been named his successor, his careful expression revealing nothing. Without comment, he turned and led them to his office and gave them chairs. He himself remained standing, on spread legs, arms crossed and massive head shot forward as he listened wordlessly to what Cumming had to say.

"Just a minute," he interrupted suddenly. Jerking about, he strode to a cupboard and flung it open; pointed to the pile of books and papers stacked within. "There," he said, "are the court records I'm supposed to have burnt! You're free to examine them. And I can answer every other charge that's been made against me."

Steve Corey asked him quietly, "The Fancher train, Brigham?"

Sharp eyes drilled into him. "I once counted you a friend of mine," said Young.

"I hope you'll believe that I tried to save that company. I swear to you I did! My people were anxious and disturbed over word of the army that was coming — and just at that time, the rumors began. It was said the Fancher people, moving through our Territory, had made all kinds of threats. They claimed to have the gun that killed Joseph Smith, and said they'd be back from California with a second army, to hit us from the rear. Maybe some of them did make such talk — I don't know. But at any rate, I had an idea there might be trouble and I sent specific orders that the train was not to be harmed. I was too late!"

"You don't know who actually did the killing?"

Brigham shook his head. "Only suspicions. I'm trying to find proof."

Steve looked at Governor Cumming, then. He saw the man's thoughtful nod.

"I'm willing to believe that, Mr. Young," the governor said. "There seems to have been misunderstanding and thoughtless violence, on both ides, from the beginning. I want to know if we can't hit upon some formula that will settle our differences, and end this rebellion."

"There has been no rebellion!" Young

retorted, with anger. "Only the illegal entry of an army into peaceable territory!"

Cumming accepted the correction gracefully. "Let's not quarrel over a word!" he said. "Suppose we withdraw the charge of rebellion, and grant amnesty to all of your militia who took part in raiding our columns and supply trains: will you, in return, show your good faith by allowing General Johnston's army to enter the Basin without a fight?"

Young frowned, holding back. "An army," he objected, "brings evils with it — drunkenness, and gambling, and the kind of women who follow the camps. We've never had such things here!"

"I'll do everything in my power to prevent it. Designate a camp site, and I'll also guarantee the city itself will not be occupied, or molested."

"All right!" said Brigham, in quick decision. "On those terms we can make peace. Fail them, and we'll fight you to the end."

"Good enough." Cumming rose to offer his hand. "As Governor of the Territory of Utah, I accept those conditions."

Brigham Young stiffened, eyeing the fleshy hand and reluctant to take it; the struggle was plain in this man who for so many years had been the autocratic master of the Territory — who had brought his people here, and built this city, and now must give up his leadership to a Gentile. But he put his own hand into Cumming's, and the agreement was sealed.

Steve Corey was already on his feet. There were details to be worked out now, and reduced to writing, but the main outline of peace had been achieved and he knew a drained, tired satisfaction. He started for the office door, thinking himself forgotten; but Brigham Young's voice stopped and turned him back.

"Corey, we have a lot of draft stock that belongs to your employer — stock our militia ran off. Every head will be returned. As for the wagons we had to destroy — that wasn't our choosing."

Steve nodded. "I understand."

"Once this mess is straightened out, we're going to need freight here, and lots of it. I'll be willing to discuss a long-term contract with Martin Wilcox; that should help to square the damage we've caused him."

Steve hardly knew how to answer this generous dismissal of grievances. He said only, "I appreciate it, Brigham. You don't owe me anything, or Martin either. I want to say thanks, for both of us!"

Governor Cumming put in, as he turned to leave, "I'll be seeing you, of course, before I leave to take the terms to Johnston?"

Corey hesitated, but answered with a shake of the head. "I'm afraid not, Governor. You don't need me any longer; and there's someone I've got to find, if I have to scour this whole terror-stricken valley, hunting for her!"

She wasn't in the town itself. Steve felt sure of this when he went to her father's house and found it shuttered and locked. Both her parents were old and in poor health; certainly Melissa would have been anxious to see them out of the town, and in a safe place. Where that place might be he couldn't know for sure, and he had no one he could ask.

But then he remembered there was a cousin living in one of the southern settlements, over two hundred miles away, a long and futile ride if he happened to be wrong. But the idea of seeing Melissa for this one last time — to make sure that all was well with her — had taken on the blind nature of a compulsion. Even if she was not at Parowan, the cousin might know where he could find her. His mind was already made up before he had half considered the arguments.

His own piebald gelding was badly jaded, and Salt Lake City appeared empty of horses. He hunted around, however, until he managed to find another, a knot-headed buckskin that looked as though it had some miles in it. Its owner was fleeing the city and did not want to trade for Steve's tired animal, but persuasion and a sizeable cash boot changed his mind. Steve paid him, switched his saddle and his trail supplies to the buckskin, and without thinking of his own condition swung astride and headed southward.

But exhaustion, protesting the tyranny of an overtaxed body, hit him and knocked him from the saddle. He camped by the trail, and was still bone-tired when he woke in a chill dawn and forced himself back onto his horse. The knife-cut in his side was bothering again. He rode into gray sage desert, with distant curtains of red-rock hills across the barren land. And increasingly, he overtook other traffic, the last stragglers of the frantic exodus from the north.

These were women, mostly, and children, and they showed the hardship this past winter had borne upon the Saints. Cut off from the world, all their supplies of food and clothing must have long since given out; for the refugees wore hungry looks and some were even barefooted. A few times Steve wasted effort trying to reassure them that the trouble was ended and they had no need for flight, but they listened without belief and he soon gave it up. He rode past the pathetic stragglers, halting only when there was some aid that he could give — and searching their faces constantly, always mindful that one of these dirty, ragged women could be Melissa.

This held him back, kept him champing at the bit over the time he lost. The monotonous miles dragged past. A second night, and a third; then the red rim of southern highlands cut the horizon ahead. He came down a timbered flank of the Black Mountains into a long valley of red sand and bunch grass, rabbit grass and greasewood and sage, and here, a miserable straggle of wood and 'dobe, was the village.

A colony had been sent, years ago, to cultivate the valley so that nearby coal and iron deposits could be worked; when these failed, the forgotten settlement had languished and nearly died. Steve knew nobody in Parowan, had no idea where to look. He rode past a scatter of encamped refugees, hunting someone that looked like a native, and finally located a sad-looking man who lounged in front of a dilapidated store-building, soaking up the sunlight. Reining in here, he shifted his cramped saddle position to ask, "Could you direct me to someone named Tyler, friend?"

The man gave him a dreary stare and shake of head. "Not in this town — and I know everybody in it!"

"You're sure?"

A deep weight of futility and frustration settled on him. He shrugged, would have turned away, except that the man went on in his hangdog voice, "Come to think of it, I'm minded that Tom Forrester's second missus was a Tyler, before they was sealed."

"Where would I find the Forresters?" Steve demanded impatiently, and receiving his directions thanked the man with a nod. He rode on then, looking for the house. When he found it, there was little to distinguish it from the others; but in the yard a woman was at work, taking wash down from a line. Steve pulled in to watch in silence for a long time, as she reached to pull clothespins and shoved clean garments into the basket at her feet.

The woman was Melissa, and Steve

thought surely the pound of his heart would make her turn and notice him.

Then he swung stiffly down, and the creak of his saddle gear did reach her ears and bring her head around. At once she turned white as the sheet on the line behind her. Staring, her breast lifting tremulously under the cheap homespun of her dress, she stood as he walked slowly toward her. Steve halted, not touching her, his hands at his sides. He said, "I was beginning to think I'd never find you."

She stammered, so low he scarcely heard her: "There's something you don't —"

"I know. You and Dan." He answered the question in her eyes: "I heard it last winter — from your brother."

"Then why are you here?"

"I've asked myself that. There's no answer. Maybe I had to have one last look, before I gave you up. Maybe I just couldn't believe, until I heard it from your lips — saw it with my own eyes. Dan Fox's wife!" The misery in her face brought him a step nearer. "How could you do it?" he demanded. "It was a mistake; you must have known that. If you didn't, surely you know it now!"

"Steve! Please!"

Resolution failed him. Suddenly his

hands were on her shoulders, drawing her savagely against him. "Can you say you love him? No, don't turn your eyes away. I want to see them when you answer!"

She would not look at him. Her head dropped forward, and her words were muffled. "He's a good man, Steve. And he's of my own people. He'd never hurt me."

"The way I did, you mean? You're still thinking of what I said about that Mountain Meadow business. But I tell you, I've changed since then! I've talked to Brigham; I'm not so sure as I was that he and the other leaders were to blame. Doesn't that make any difference?"

"How could it, now? I'm sealed to Dan."

"No!" Refusal to accept what he knew was so, gripped and blinded him; only Melissa's sob of pain made him aware that his tightened hands were shaking and hurting her.

"I'm sorry," he said finally. "You were right. There *is* a barrier between us, always was. One that Fate put there, and another we were blind enough to build ourselves. Now, it's too late!" He stepped back, and with an effort put his glance on hers. "I wish you every happiness, you and Dan. Please believe that!"

"Oh, Steve!" He saw that she was on the

verge of crying, her mouth tremulous. "You — you'll find a girl, someday — better for you than I would have been. Someone of your own faith."

He didn't answer except with the hard twist of his bitter smile. Instead he told her, "I'd like a word with Dan before I go."

"He isn't here. Dan and Orson both volunteered to stay behind with those who are to set the fires, if Salt Lake City falls to the Gentiles."

"But you hadn't heard the news, then! There's been a settlement, Melissa. The war is over!"

Unbelief tempered the joy that came into her look. "You mean the army's going back?"

"Not quite that. Terms have been arranged to let them enter the Basin without fighting, and call quits on everything that's already happened." He saw her eyes cloud, and frowned. "You don't like it, do you? You can't see anything but evil in any Gentile!"

"I'm sorry."

But there was nothing to be said. They stood looking at each other a moment. Then Steve lifted his shoulders on a long breath. "Good-by, Melissa."

He heeled around and started from her,

holding himself stiffly against the futile temptation to turn again and make some final plea. He might have managed to ride away without looking back, but now something brought his attention to the adjoining yard. There near the fence a child in a dirty pinafore was grubbing with a broken piece of stick — a golden-haired little girl. Something jarred him, made him halt in mid-stride to look more closely. He heard Melissa exclaim, "What is it, Steve? What's the matter?"

Half turning back, he said sharply: "That little girl — I've seen her before."

"Why, it's her aunt's house," Melissa told him, obviously puzzled at his manner. "I believe she was sent down from Salt Lake City to stay last year when all the trouble started. A strange child. She won't talk to anyone. She acts almost as though she were frightened."

A name broke from him, then. "Sally! Sally Owen!" And he saw the child lift her head.

Melissa exclaimed, "I don't understand —"

Quickly he vaulted the low fence; when he went down onto his ankles beside her, a wave of terror crossed the little girl's face and she drew back from him. "Don't be afraid!" he said quickly. "I'm your friend, Sally!" And getting no response he continued, with quiet persistence: "Don't you know me, honey? We met last summer. You were with the wagon train — you and your mother and daddy. You picked some flowers. . . ."

Unable to contain herself, Melissa broke in. "What wagon train? What are you talking about?"

He gave her a hurried shake of the head, and turned back to the little girl. Still there was no sign of recollection, no change in her manner. "I gave you a ride on my horse," he went on. "And I guessed your name."

That brought the first sign of life to the shadowed eyes. Sally's head lifted, and he saw disbelief struggle with a sudden pleased recollection. She got the word out with a real effort: "Steve?"

"That's right, honey — that's fine!" He started to place a hand upon her tangled curls, then, but he moved too soon; fear ran across her face again and she cringed away from him. He withdrew the hand, quickly. He forced patience, knowing it could not be easy to break through this shell that horror had built around her.

He said, in the same kind and soothing

273

voice, "Yes, honey. I'm Steve. I'm not going to let anything hurt you, not anything. That's a promise!" He paused, letting his words soak into her mind, and added gently: "So don't be afraid. You won't be afraid any more, will you?"

She swallowed, and tried to smile faintly as she repeated, "Steve." And this time when he reached out his hand she did not cringe from it, but let him place it upon her arm.

"Now!" he exclaimed. "That's a lot better!" He didn't want to press her too hard, but he could not hold the questions back. "Maybe you'll tell me what you're doing here. Where are your folks?" He thought she wasn't going to answer. Terror flooded her eyes again, and for a moment she seemed about to retreat behind the shield of fear.

But then she told him, solemnly, "My daddy and mommy are dead."

"Steve!" exclaimed Melissa. "Will you please tell me what this is all about?"

He looked up at her. "This little girl was in the Fancher train, that was destroyed at Mountain Meadow. I can't imagine how she managed to stay alive — but at last, now, we have a chance to learn exactly what happened that day. Whether it was

Indians, or white men —"

Sally Owen broke in, her childish voice trembling. "It was a white man came to the wagons with a piece of cloth on a stick. He said if Daddy and the others would give him their guns, he'd make the Indians go away. So Mr. Fancher said we'd do it, and the white men came and some of them took all the mommas and the children, and some of them took the daddies, and we started walking away from the wagons. But then the men — they —" Her face twisted in remembered horror, and she began to cry.

Steve heard Melissa's shaken voice. "She's — only a baby, Steve! You can't take her word —"

"Can't you?" He gathered Sally into his arms and straightened, with the little girl clinging to him as to the only friend who could protect her from her memories. A woman had come from the door of the house, and the whiteness of her face told him that she had heard. Steve met her with a look that was ice-cold. "Are you ready to explain?"

The woman was middle-aged, her drab hair streaked with gray. As she hesitated to answer, Melissa said quickly, "I told him what you said, Mrs. Peters — that she was sent down to you from the north."

"Yes," Steve said. "But now I think you'd better tell the truth!"

The woman wore a stricken look. Her thin hands worked at the material of her apron, and her throat swelled with the words that did not want to come. "It was — your brother, Melissa," she stammered. "Orson brought her!"

At the understanding that welled into Melissa's stricken eyes, then, Steve could have wished he had let this alone, had never forced it to the light. Melissa's hands gripped the fence pickets. "It — it couldn't be!" she gasped. "He must have found her! Isn't that so, honey?" She turned anxiously to the child in Corey's arms. "It only happened a few miles from here. He found you and brought you where you'd be safe. Isn't that what happened?"

But Sally Owen shook her head frantically. "No, no, no! *He killed my mommy!*"

"And then his nerve failed him, I guess," Steve Corey added into the sudden silence, holding her trembling little body tight. "Something decent broke through the bloodlust and told him he couldn't kill the child too — that if he spared her she'd be too young to accuse him."

"He made me swear I'd never tell!" the

woman stammered. "He knew I'd always wanted a child. I didn't ask questions. I said just what he told me to. I never meant no harm." She was beginning to weep hysterically.

"I — don't believe it!" But the conviction drained from Melissa's voice even as the words were spoken, and Steve did not answer her.

"Mrs. Peters," he said, "I'm leaving Sally with you, for now at least. Later, if she has folks still living in Arkansas, I'll see that she's sent home to them."

The little girl clutched at him. "Don't go away!"

"I have to, honey," he told her soothingly. "But you'll be all right. And I'll come back for you when I've found this man."

"I'm going with you, Steve," Melissa said, and though the tragedy still darkened her eyes, her voice was steady, her manner calmed now and determined. "Orson has never lied to me. If this is the truth, he'll tell me! But I can't believe it until he does."

Steve looked at her soberly. The first impulse, to refuse, gave way before the realization that he could not do so. He nodded. "He's your brother; you have the right. We'll be starting back tomorrow morning — early. Be ready to ride."

# 17

The smell of spring was strong upon the land tonight, like a promise; even the wind seemed to have lost something of its harshness. Steve shoved fuel into the campfire, stood a moment staring into it. He lifted his glance to the sky and to the outline of a distant run cutting black across the lower stars. Nearby, Melissa stirred, and he turned and looked at her, curled in her blankets, the fire between her and the place where he had spread his own bed.

He thought. *The last night. . . .*

These few days alone with her had held their poignant sweetness, even though they had spoken little during all the long ride, weighted by thought of their purpose and of what waited for them tomorrow when they reached their destination. Then he would deliver her to her husband, to Dan Fox. And the showdown which must come with Orson Tyler would drop the final curtain on whatever tenderness had ever existed between him and this girl.

The unfairness of it, and his longing for

her, swelled in him suddenly and in a couple of strides he was standing over her. Her face was turned toward him, the lips a little parted. His breathing harshened to the pull of desire, that brought him suddenly to one knee. His hand fumbled at the blanket, his mouth ready to stop hers with his demanding kiss when she should rouse, startled and afraid.

Then he saw that her eyes had opened, and she looked into his face without alarm, the sleep slowly fading from her. She asked, then, "Steve? Is anything wrong?"

"No." He forced the word out, and followed it with others equally clumsy. "I wondered if you were comfortable, is all. It's a cold night."

She smiled a little drowsily. "I'm all right. Thank you, Steve."

The coldness was gone from her eyes. He saw in them tenderness, and trust, and regret. And that she still loved him; a male awareness whispered the certainty that he could take her now, if he would.

He said gruffly, "Good night!" and stumbled to his feet. His legs shook so violently he felt they could scarcely support him. He turned away from the girl, and he could feel his nails digging into his palms, in the effort to steady himself.

For there was more than this moment. There would be the lifelong aftermath of shame, that would turn even the memory of the love they had had so briefly into bitterness. He would not do this to her. Yet he knew now — he *knew* — that despite the muddled confusion of events too great for them, which had torn their lives asunder, Melissa loved him still.

Given the time they could not have, their love might have surmounted every barrier that came between. Every barrier, that is, except the one which had in fact risen to separate them forever: their own basic decency, and respect for Dan Fox, who had married her, and who loved her too.

That, it was too late for either of them to change.

The tide of refugees for the southern settlements had thinned, now; and at last it ceased and the road lay wholly deserted. From this Steve had known that Salt Lake City must have emptied itself, and so he had been a little prepared for what he was to find here; after all, the work of evacuation had been nearly half completed when he entered the city, days ago, with Governor Cumming. Even so, riding into the silent and stricken place gave him an awed feeling of being in the presence of death.

Here were the houses, and the wide streets, and the eerie heapings of straw and tinder which a few sulphur matches and a carrying wind could turn into a giant, crackling bonfire. Yet here was no sight or sound of life except the muffled echoes of their own hootbeats, the skulking figure of a dog that crossed the street somewhere ahead.

Melissa said, in a hushed voice, "It looks so awful! Like a city that has died —"

Her eyes, stricken, appealed to him for comfort, and he had to steel himself to keep from putting out a hand to touch her. He said, gently, "Try not to think like that. I know how you feel, but everything will be the same again." He was rewarded by a smile that did not quite touch her eyes.

He said then: "I wonder where we look for your brother, and Dan?"

She could only shake her head, helplessly. They drifted on through the haunted, empty streets working toward the heart of the city, watching the doorways and the vacant windows for a hint of movement, any sign of the other human beings they knew must be somewhere in the town. All was orderly; evidently there had been no looting.

And then they both heard, at almost the same instant, a growing swell of sound somewhere to the north of them.

It's meaning was entirely unclear, at first. On a common impulse the man and the girl drew rein, as she whispered sharply, "Listen!" He nodded, to indicate that he heard. Frowning, he began to make out its individual elements — the slow thud of hoofs and grind of wheels, coming closer, and the whisper of many boots without rhythm. Suddenly he knew what the sounds signified.

"Come on!" he grunted. They lifted their horses into a canter that carried them briskly ahead. And at a wide street crossing they halted, to watch the Utah Expedition pass through Salt Lake City.

This army came not as conquerors, but at route step with arms slung, tired from the long march. They came in a strange silence. Field guns rattled past, and supply wagons, the big wheels jouncing over the rough street and lifting dust. There was no halt anywhere; the long line of men and horses and equipment moved steadily, noiselessly on.

Steve felt Melissa's hand tighten on his sleeve, and looking at her found her eyes on his in disbelief and a dawning wonder.

"What you told me was the truth!" she exclaimed. "They're passing straight through. They're keeping their word not to occupy the city."

For answer he pointed to a horseman who rode slowly by in the drifting dust, bared head bowed. "See that man? That's Colonel Cooke," he told her. "He commanded the Mormon Battalion in the War with Mexico, and he always said they were the finest fighting men he ever led. Look at him! D'you think there's any triumph in his heart, at this moment?"

"I was wrong, Steve!" she said humbly. "We all were! We never had anything to fear!"

He spoke gently. "You couldn't have known that. I thought you were unreasonable, to turn against me because of the part I figured I had to take. I figured it was loyalty I owed a friend, but you had been my friends, too, and now you saw your whole world threatened by the forces I stood with. Somehow, I didn't understand that — or understand how you could look on me as a traitor." He shook his head, his mouth quirked in a smile of irony. "Now the trouble's over, I guess it's easier for us to see where we both made mistakes!"

Her lower lip trembled. "Oh, Steve! I —"

"We've got a job to do," he reminded her, not letting her finish what might be better left unspoken. "Shall we ride and find your husband?"

"Yes," she said.

They reined about, putting their backs to the drifting dust and flowing river of sound; and it was then that Steve noticed a man who stood back in the shadow of a doorway, also watching the tide of marching troops. Steve angled his horse across the empty street, leaning to peer beneath the porch overhang. The half-seen figure started to withdraw from sight, but when he called, "Hey, you! Wait a minute!" the man opened the door wider and edged out suspiciously. "Do you know a man named Orson Tyler?" Steve demanded, and getting a blank look added, "Or Dan Fox?"

Recognition showed in the other's face at that name. He demanded sharply. "What about him?"

Steve indicated the woman. "This is Mrs. Fox. She's got to find him. It's very important."

"Oh." An arm and a pointing hand came out of the shadows. "Look over that way a couple of blocks, you might find him there."

"Thanks!"

They kept to the side streets where all was as still as before, though at intersections they could catch a glimpse of the passing army. When they found the designated block of houses, it looked as empty and as lifeless as any other. Steve pulled rein in the middle of the street, ran his glance along the blank house fronts.

"Dan Fox!" he shouted. He repeated the call but despaired of an answer, until the screech of an opening window pulled his head around.

A second-story window had been run up; he saw the gleam of a gun, and Dan's face staring in astonishment and alarm. "Melissa!" the man exclaimed, recognizing his wife. "What is this?"

"We're looking for Orson," she called up to him. "Have you seen him anywhere?"

"He's here with me."

The head was withdrawn. Steve and Melissa rode over and swung down before the house. As they mounted to the porch, the door was thrown open and Dan rushed out to them. He had a gun thrust behind the belt of his trousers, and he was unshaven and appeared tight with strain.

He murmured his wife's name and embraced her quickly and passionately; Steve thought she submitted without real pleasure. He looked quickly away, and when he turned back saw Dan's puzzled and suspicious eyes on him. Afterward Dan Fox glanced up and down the street, as though hunting danger; and with his arm about Melissa, he led the way inside.

Steve entered after them, closing the door, and found himself in a room darkened by drawn shades. The house had been hurriedly vacated by its occupants; there was an overturned chair, and drawers left opened after valuables had been removed. The place shared the air of dread and waiting that hung over this whole city and was reflected in Dan's murky stare.

Steve asked him, a little shortly. "What are you hiding from?"

Fox had released his wife; he turned angrily to this man who had been his friend and rival. "From the Gentiles, of course!"

"You don't need to, any longer," Melissa told him breathlessly. "We've been watching them; they'll do no harm. They're going straight through the city as they promised. Listen, and you can hear them!"

"I can hear them, all right!" he retorted savagely. "And until every soldier and caisson has come and gone, I'll be watching for the first hint of treachery!"

"Oh, Dan!" she protested. "Haven't we

been blind long enough? Why must we go on clinging to suspicions that have already caused so much hatred?"

He did not answer her. His cold gaze had turned on Steve and he said, "Corey, I'm waiting to learn what you're doing here!"

The stairs creaked behind them. Orson Tyler, thin and gaunted since the last time Steve had seen him, came slowly down; he still favored the leg hurt in the supply-train raid last winter. Like Dan he was stubble-bearded, and the wild look Corey had seen on him that day in the sleet-slashed woods was even more pronounced, like a feverish fire that lighted his eyes. He carried a cap-and-ball pistol, hanging straight down toward the faded runner carpeting the stairs. Not quite at the bottom he paused, to stare at his sister and the two men in the room below.

Steve said quietly, "My business isn't with you, Dan," and started past him toward the stairs. But Melissa, turning quickly, laid a hand on his shoulder.

"No — please! I want to do the talking!"

In spite of himself he stopped, nodding. He could imagine what was in her heart as she moved to face this brother of hers, a year or two older than she, yet somehow always emotionally less mature.

"Orson —" She began, and her voice choked. "We just came from Parowan. We saw the little girl you brought there. We —"

Her voice died at the startling alteration in him. His head jerked back, his eyes darkened, his mouth drew tight against the bones of his face. Steve Corey could not hold himself in. "Any need of making her go on with this?" he challenged. "I guess you know what she means. You haven't the nerve to deny it!"

"It *isn't* true?" Melissa was pleading with her brother, now, begging for some assurance she could believe. "You weren't at Mountain Meadow?"

"What if I was?" He shouted it back at her, in a sudden fury. "Somebody had to take the responsibility. Otherwise they'd have got clear away from us, *unpunished!*"

Stricken, Melissa could not speak. But Dan Fox strode forward, and his look was black with thunder. "What are you saying?"

"You don't know what it was like in Parowan, last fall when that train came though — poisoning springs, and stealing, and violating women?"

Steve cut in on him. "Just a minute! Did you actually *know* any of this for fact? Did

288

you see any of it?" The youngster's look was answer enough. "Of course not! You listened to some kind of wild rumor, didn't you? You believed what some hotheaded fool told you! Who in the world spread such filth?"

"Why —" Orson stammered a little, losing some of his fanatic sureness under the probing. "The man I talked to was a stranger. A redheaded man, with a patchy beard and his face all scarred —"

The description of Bill Reno staggered Corey. He heard the trembling in his own voice. "You listened to *him?* And then went and butchered helpless — ?"

"Damn you, shut up!"

The sound was between a scream and a sob — the cry, Steve realized suddenly, of a cruelly tortured conscience. And, with the need to silence his tormentor, Orson all at once swept up the gun that he held at his side.

Melissa gasped, but Steve Corey was already in motion. He lunged forward, hurled himself at the legs of the man who stood above him, and staggered Orson back into the balustrade. Steve's boot struck the edge of a step and drove him upward; his hand groped for Orson's gun wrist and, finding it, cracked the arm hard against the railing. The pistol fell from the lad's numbed fingers, dropped to the floor.

Orson lost balance and fell, as Steve, moving back, pawed at the hair that had fallen into his eyes. Corey looked down in mingled contempt and pity at this young man who lay sprawled and panting; but Dan Fox was not finished with him. He shoved Steve aside, reached for a handful of Orson's clothing and dragged him to his feet, propped him against the newel post. "Now, talk!" he ordered, in a hard and terrible voice. "Tell us everything. Who was in it with you?"

Orson was sweating, all the hardness gone out of him. He swabbed a trembling hand across his face. "We made a pact that none of us would ever —"

Dan twisted a hand into the front of his brother-in-law's shirt. "You hear me? I want a name! I want to know who planned that butchery!" And getting no answer from the boy, Dan hit him.

The blow was a sharp, slapping sound in the quiet of the closed-up house; Melissa screamed as though it had struck her own flesh. She spun away, directly into the hands of Steve Corey who clutched her to him, and felt her body wince as a second heavy blow sounded.

"Who was in it?" Dan repeated in a savage voice that didn't sound like his.

"John Lee!" sobbed Orson. "Isaac Haight . . . Sam McMurdy. . . ." The dike broken, the names poured from him like a flood.

"Not Brigham Young? Or the other Church leaders?"

"Brigham's an old woman; we acted without him. The Indians were supposed to do it all, but they botched things; and we had to finish. Lee went in under a truce flag and got their guns. Then we —"

"Hold it!" snapped Steve. "We want to get all this on paper, Dan, while he's willing to talk. It'll be needed for the trial."

Dan nodded, his rage cooling. But Melissa, breaking from Steve's arms, peered anxiously into his face. "Not by the army, though! Oh, please, Steve! It isn't only that he's my brother," she went on quickly, seeing his shake of head. "It's your turn to show if you have any faith at all in us. We've admitted our mistakes; now let our people prove we don't condone such things. Let the Church condemn and punish the ones who did it!"

He looked down at her, his own face feeling stiff and wooden. He looked at Dan, and at the sobbing creature huddled against the newel post.

Steve lifted his shoulders in a shrug. "He's all yours!" he said, and turned abruptly and walked out of the house.

# 18

Bill Reno! York Baggett's man!

He remembered now that day in the Leavenworth office — Martin Wilcox repeating everything Corey had told him about the Fancher train and the trouble that might come to it on entering Mormon territory. Baggett had listened, without expression. And on that very night Bill Reno had ridden west on some unnamed mission.

Dead, Reno could not even be forced to explain. Fury swept through Steve, and settled into purpose. He walked out to his horse, checked the cinches, and swung astride. A few blocks away an army still passed through the hushed city. He pulled about, meaning to ride in that direction.

And that was when he saw the smoke.

Steve Corey went up in the stirrups, staring without belief at the ugly stains against the clear sky — black, billowing eruptions that told of the flames at work beneath. For a second he seemed unable to move; then with a hoarse shout he kicked the buckskin's flank and the animal leaped ahead.

He had a start of a couple of hundred yards before he thought of Dan Fox, realizing that if a fire had broken out among the tinder-banked houses of the deserted city, he couldn't combat it alone. Still, there were the military, who would quickly see the smoke if they had not already; and that was as much help as he could need. So he plunged on, pounding along vacant streets between the sightless rows of buildings, taking the corners with savage jerks of the rein that almost spilled the horse. Within minutes he heard the crackle of the fires, and after that he saw them, and felt their heat.

Through a smoky haze laced with embers, he looked along the throat of a block of small, frame houses. Three were burning, at intervals along one side of the street; another had just started across the way. From the pattern he would have known that the fires were set, even if he had not smelled the reek of burning oil, or seen the dark figures moving about them.

A gunshot cracked, and out in the middle of the street he saw a horse rear and with a scream of pain fall heavily, throwing its rider. The man lit rolling, reached his knees; he had a gun in his hand and, crouching, he put a bullet into the one who had shot his horse. Steve, spurring in, saw now that the man kneeling by the dead mount was Ed Loman.

Not far from Corey, back turned to him, another stood over a spilled tin of oil and leveled his cap-and-ball pistol for a dead bead on the young fellow in the street. Steve gave a jerk of the reins that swerved the buckskin directly toward this man. The latter heard, and was twisting to get out of the way when the horse ran him down, spilled him caroming off one heavy shoulder. The gun was knocked from his hand; he hit the ground heavily and lay still. Glancing at him briefly from the saddle, Steve recognized one of the tough Wilcox & Baggett wagon crew.

Out in the street Ed was calling and gesticulating wildly. "Back there, Steve! It's Baggett!"

He was running as he yelled but Steve, spurring, quickly left him behind. Embers from the bonfires and burning building sailed about him. He pulled left around one of the torched buildings and plunged into the passageway between it and the still-intact house adjoining; but a quick down-draft smothered him in reeking, oily smoke shot with flames, and at once he was having trouble with his horse.

The frightened animal would not give to the reins; it screamed and reared and tossed its head, frenzied by fear. After a futile moment Steve, cursing, slid out of the saddle, let it go, and plunged ahead on foot. Smoke blinded him utterly but he went straight through, running. Then, as suddenly as it had descended, the smoke lifted again and he saw Baggett.

He had tried to warn this man, once, of what the impact of the frontier could do to him. Now, York Baggett had lost the last traces of gentility. His clothing hung shapeless on him, and his face was hard-stubbled and smoke-blackened. He was busy sloshing liquid from a can onto the wall of a house and the tinder piled against it. He scarcely glanced at the man coming toward him through the threads of oily smoke, as he shouted harshly across a shoulder: "This is enough to keep the army busy a few minutes. We'll head for Temple Square!"

Then he saw Steve Corey, and knew him. Rage swept his face; he threw aside his empty fuel tin and groped for a weapon.

Drunk as he was, Baggett was not too

drunk for danger. But Steve had to think first of Jud Noonan, whom he glimpsed now a dozen paces to his left. Noonan's gun was already out and rising. Steve pivoted, slashing his gunbarrel around, and fired directly at the man's blocky shape.

He had never tried a more frantic shot, and he was frankly astonished to see the big man jerk as the ball struck him. Noonan's bearded face turned expressionless; his body lost stiffness and began to take the curious shape of a man crumpling to a fall. Steve turned back to meet the flash of Baggett's belt gun. It seemed to explode, blindingly, in his very face. He did not feel the hat leave his head. His thumb was on the prong of his own gun hammer, rolling it back with practiced ease, rotating a fresh cap into place beneath the pin. His whole hand squeezed upon the trigger and butt, properly; and the gun's recoil struck his palm even as York Baggett fought his weapon back down into aim.

It was done as quickly as that.

Still a little numbed by the speed of things, Steve was standing over the bodies of the men he had killed when Ed Loman came running through the drifting smoke. Ed's face was white with shock. "Steve! You all right?"

He had picked up Corey's fallen hat from the ground and Steve, taking it from him, saw the bullethole punched through the crown. For the first time, he felt a sick aftermath of danger.

Ed looked at York Baggett's still form, his mouth hardened with loathing. He touched a lifeless hand with his boot toe and said, in a hard voice, "Scum!"

After that, a constraint of silence suddenly lay upon these two. Steve Corey looked at the younger man, who kept his eyes on the ground and would not bring them up again to the face of the one who had been his friend. With an effort he found his voice.

"Ed —"

"No, Steve!" Ed blurted, rushing it out. "Let me say my piece first. I been hoping for the chance, ever since that day when I socked you. I'm sorry for that," he went on, miserably. "A friendship — it's something you can't let break up, just because both parties to it might happen to want the same girl."

"But I don't want your girl, Ed!" Steve answered him. "It was only woman-hunger, nothing to be proud of, but at least I didn't let it go to a point where I never could have forgiven myself! You had every right to be sore about it. Bobby's a fine girl, Ed. She loves you a lot. And if you love her —" His voice edged with bitterness, "— don't let anybody take her away from you. Not anybody — for any reason!"

His tone brought him Ed's look of puzzled sympathy, but he did not explain his meaning. He laid a hand against his friend's shoulder, briefly; then turned and walked quickly away, into the street that seemed filled now with blue-clad troops bringing the threatened fire under control.

Someone had caught his frightened horse and tied it, out of danger of the drifting brands. Steve spoke soothingly to settle it, and then swung to its back. He saw the spare, stern figure watching operations from saddle a few rods along the street, and he put the buckskin that way. General Johnston looked about as he rode alongside.

"A couple of dead men back there, General," Steve said with a jerk of his head. "I killed them. York Baggett and his friend Noonan. They set this fire, and then meant to torch Temple Square while we were busy fighting to put it out. If they'd succeeded, there'd have been no question of the Saints ever calling it quits until they were beaten. There'd have been a war, for fair — and further profits for York Baggett!"

The general said nothing for a long minute; his sharp glance rested on Steve, but Corey had a feeling the man was scarcely seeing him, absorbing instead the meaning of what he had been told. Then, subtly, Johnston's expression altered and a kind of tiredness came into his eyes, the set of his mouth, the very lines of his soldier's body.

He said, in a voice so low that Steve scarcely heard him above the surrounding confusion: "Let us hope and pray that we have had our fill of war!"

Steve nodded. "I'll second that!"

Yet even as he spoke, it was as though he heard, in his mind, the echo of other voices — angry voices, building to a clamor and crescendo of hatred; and, against this ugly background, certain things that he had heard York Baggett say about the coming inevitable war over slavery, between North and South. Words that he had listened to, hating them and the man who spoke them, yet finding in them the dreaded ring of truth.

In a strange, calm moment of premonition, he looked at the general sitting saddle here amid drifting smoke and the excited yelling of his troops, and for this moment it might, strangely, have been a different setting. A battleground, perhaps, of that war which waited in the future — and in which, if it came, he and this Kentuckian would undoubtedly find themselves on different sides.

Steve frowned, and shook his head to free it of this vision. But it remained to haunt him for long minutes after he had ridden on, leaving Johnston, and the smoky and littered street behind him.

He had no wish at all to go near Melissa and her husband again, but if they had seen the pall of smoke he knew they would be concerned about it; it was only common decency to stop for a moment, at least, and tell them the danger was over. So he turned at the street where he had left them, and where Melissa's horse still stood tied before the house.

He reined in, swung stiffly down and went up to the porch. His hand was raised, ready to knuckle the closed and silent door, when the gunshot sounded within.

For a count of seconds he could not have moved; then his right hand remembered the familiar shape of his holstered pistol, and was reaching for it as his left struck the latch of the door and his shoulder drove it open. He stumbled with the suddenness of his rush, falling in across the threshold. As he recovered balance, the first face he saw was Orson Tyler's.

Wild-eyed, Orson had been running for the door when it slammed open and he checked himself, staring at the man who stood there. The gun in his hand was smoking from the shot Steve had heard. Now, his face twisting, he brought it up and punched out a bullet. Steve felt the lead strike his shoulder; at that point-blank distance it hurled him, hard, against the jamb of the opened door.

He almost lost his gun, and it was a moment before he could recover. He expected a second bullet, but the stumbling clatter of feet on the stairs told him that instead of rushing the street door Orson was taking to another way of escape. Maybe he had lost his head; or maybe he knew there was a rear staircase, and another exit.

But all wonder about the young man's intentions was jarred from Steve for the moment, because he had discovered the crumpled shape of Dan Fox, and Melissa on her knees beside her husband. Aware of the thawing of his shoulder wound, the seep of blood down his arm, he swayed a little as he walked toward them. He looked down at Dan Fox, dumbly; the stricken glance Melissa gave him would have told him the truth, even without sight of the bullet wound in Dan's lifeless chest.

Half under him, as he lay, Steve saw the sheet of foolscap and its close-packed writing.

Melissa said, in a strangled voice, "Orson got the gun away, and —" Grief and horror choked her.

Still without a word, Steve Corey turned toward the stairs. He moved slowly, for the shock of the bullet had drained him of all strength and left him weak and trembling. But his gun arm was unhurt and he held his gun steady by an effort of will. At a turning of the stairwell, he came to a long hallway splitting the second floor from front to rear.

He risked a look that showed him at once this house had no rear stairs. Unless he wanted to chance a leap from a high window, then, Orson was trapped. There was no sign of him in the hall; he would be behind one of the doors that opened off it.

Steve Corey thought the pound of his heart must carry like the thud of regular drumbeats in the silent passageway. He took the last step and slid cautiously around a corner, pressed flat against the wall. His shoulder throbbed in rhythm with the throb of his pulse; his jaws were clamped tight, aching in his effort to control the pain and his own weakness.

He ran a slow, studying glance along the blank faces of the doors. There were four of them, all closed. The thought that he must try each one, with a hidden gun waiting somewhere and ready for him, was enough to start the sweat flowing. But he had no choice. He steeled himself to move forward, toward the nearest one. But even as his hand touched the knob, the click of a latch behind him made him whirl.

He guessed at once the one he wanted; crossing the carpet, he stopped to listen and heard plainly the hoarse and heavy breathing, just beyond the thin panel.

Corey moved aside, out of direct line, and bracing his feet against the faint roll of the floor under his weakened body called sharply: "Orson! I know you're in there. I'll kill you if I have to — but surrender, and I'll guarantee your chance of a fair trial, at the hands of your own Church."

The answer came, high-pitched, touched with madness: "They can't judge me! Not even old Brigham himself! He betrayed us; he made a peace with the Gentiles. No one else but me sees that there can't be any peace. We've got to fight, and keep fighting, until we've driven them out of the Basin, until we've killed them all!"

Steve understood, then, and he closed his eyes tight for a minute. "Orson," he called, feeling the itchy trickle of sweat down the stubble that shagged his cheeks. "I'm sorry as hell for you! You're a sick man. You butchered innocent men and women. For all your raving, I think you know in your heart you're wrong — you'll never justify yourself, or what you did that day at Mountain Meadow! I'm starting a count of three," he added. "Then I'm coming in to get you." He said, harshly: *"One!"*

The hoarse breathing stopped and held, on an intaken, caught breath. Steve waited, feeling the grind of the pistol butt against his tight fingers, the pain of his hurt shoulder, and the trembling in his legs. No sound at all from beyond the door.

He swallowed, in a dry and rasping throat. His voice sounded strange and unnatural to his own ears. "Two, Orson!"

He heard a single, muffled sob, and then the shot, like a roar of echoes in the thin walls of the house. But he did not fully comprehend, even yet, until he heard the slump of a body against the closed door, and the sliding whisper of scraping cloth. The fallen pistol had struck the foot of the door and now a single thread of smoke leaked through the crack below and ribboned slowly up the painted outer surface. Steve looked at the smoke for a moment; afterward, not opening the door at all, he turned and dropped his own gun into its holster as he walked away toward the head of the stairs.

He saw blood on the wall, where he had stood and leaned his hurt shoulder. And at the bottom of the steps Melissa stood waiting. In her hands was the sheet of paper — Orson's confession, and list of names. Her face drained of color, she asked the question with her eyes.

Steve came down and stood before her; he nodded. He watched the trembling of her lips as the tears started, but he knew there was strength in this girl to accept her grief, and absorb it, and pass beyond.

As though echoing his thoughts, she said, "It's best — this way. He couldn't have stood trial. Orson was weak. He —" Uncontrollably, her lips began to tremble.

"He wasn't all to blame," Steve reminded her gently. "Orson was brought up in a world of hatred. He never understood that there might be a time when Saints and Gentiles would live together peacefully. With the army's help, we're going to build that new world. We've got to have faith in it, and in ourselves."

Melissa nodded. And then suddenly she came to him, sobbing, her head against his chest; and he put his good arm gently around her and held her that way, unspeaking and undemanding, letting her take the comfort she needed from his strength, and his sure love.

# About the Author

*D(wight) B(ennett) Newton* is the author of a number of notable Western novels. Born in Kansas City, Missouri, Newton went on to complete work for a Master's degree in history at the University of Missouri. From the time he first discovered Max Brand in Street and Smith's *Western Story Magazine*, he knew he wanted to be an author of Western fiction. He began contributing Western stories and novelettes to the Red Circle group of Western pulp magazines published by Newsstand in the late 1930s. During the Second World War, Newton served in the U.S. Army Engineers and fell in love with the central Oregon region when stationed there. He would later become a permanent resident of that state and Oregon frequently serves as the locale for many of his finest novels. As a client of the August Lenniger Literary Agency, Newton found that every time he switched publishers he was given a different byline by his agent. This complicated his visibility. Yet in notable novels from *Range Boss* (1949), the first original novel ever published in a modern paperback edition, through his impressive list of titles for the Double D series from Doubleday, *The Oregon Rifles*, *Crooked River Canyon*, and *Disaster Creek* among them, he produced a very special kind of Western story. What makes it so special is the combination of characters who seem real and about whom a reader comes to care a great deal and Newton's fundamental humanity, his realization early on (perhaps because of his study of history) that little that happened in the West was ever simple but rather made desperately complicated through the conjunction of numerous opposed forces working at cross purposes. Yet, through all of the turmoil on the frontier, a basic human decency did emerge. It was this which made the American frontier experience so profoundly unique and which produced many of the remarkable human beings to be found in the world of Newton's Western fiction.

The employees of Thorndike Press hope you have enjoyed this Large Print book. All our Thorndike and Wheeler Large Print titles are designed for easy reading, and all our books are made to last. Other Thorndike Press Large Print books are available at your library, through selected bookstores, or directly from us.

For information about titles, please call:

(800) 223-1244

or visit our Web site at:

www.gale.com/thorndike
www.gale.com/wheeler

To share your comments, please write:

Publisher
Thorndike Press
295 Kennedy Memorial Drive
Waterville, ME  04901